THE SASQUATCH ESCAPE

THE IMAGINARY VETERINARY: BOOK 1

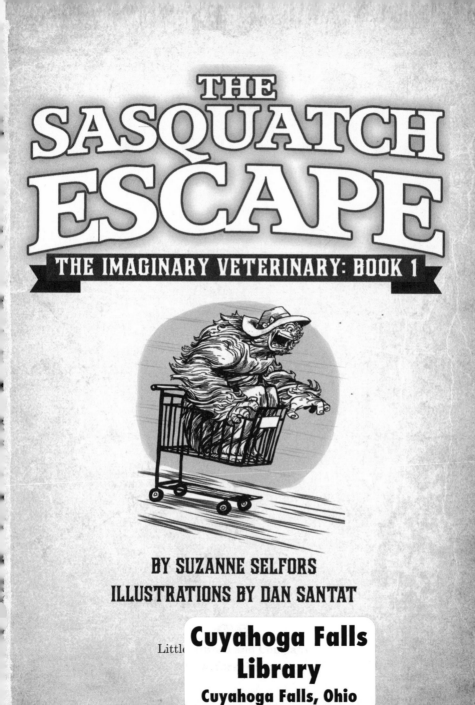

BY SUZANNE SELFORS
ILLUSTRATIONS BY DAN SANTAT

Little

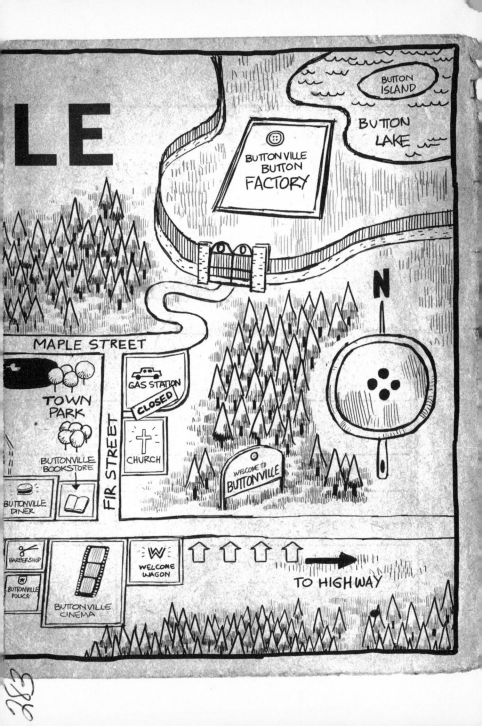

Copyright © 2013 by Suzanne Selfors
Illustrations copyright © 2013 by Dan Santat

Little, Brown and Company

Hachette Book Group
237 Park Avenue, New York, NY 10017
Visit our website at www.lb-kids.com

Little, Brown and Company is a division of Hachette Book Group, Inc.
The Little, Brown name and logo are trademarks of Hachette Book Group, Inc.

The publisher is not responsible for websites
(or their content) that are not owned by the publisher.

First Edition: April 2013

Library of Congress Cataloging-in-Publication Data

Selfors, Suzanne.
The sasquatch escape / by Suzanne Selfors ; illustrated by Dan Santat.—First edition.
     pages cm.—(The imaginary veterinary ; 1)
  Summary: Spending the summer in his grandfather's rundown town, ten-year-old Ben meets an adventurous local girl, and together they learn that the town's veterinarian runs a secret hospital for Imaginary Creatures.
ISBN 978-0-316-20934-2
  [1. Imaginary creatures—Fiction. 2. Veterinarians—Fiction.] I. Santat, Dan, illustrator. II. Title.
PZ7.S456922Sas 2013
[Fic]—dc23
2012032531

10 9 8 7 6 5 4 3 2 1

RRD-C

Printed in the United States of America

To sasquatches everywhere

CONTENTS

CHAPTER 1: *Story Bird*

CHAPTER 2: *Welcome to Buttonville*

CHAPTER 3: *The House on Pine Street*

CHAPTER 4: *Dollar Store Girl*

CHAPTER 5: *Jelly Bean Man*

CHAPTER 6: *Sea Horse Face*

CHAPTER 7: *Pearl's Promise*

CHAPTER 8: *The Old Button Factory*

CHAPTER 9: *Mr. Tabby*

CHAPTER 10: *The Wyvern*

CHAPTER 11: *Hairy Escape*

CHAPTER 12: *Sasquatch Catching Kit*

CHAPTER 13: *The Scurry*

CHAPTER 14: *Welcome Wagon*

CHAPTER 15: *Sloth Sighting*

CHAPTER 16: *Hairy Pudding*

CHAPTER 17: *Fog Day*

CHAPTER 18: *Bad Berries*

CHAPTER 19: *Hairy Return*

CHAPTER 20: *Dr. Woo*

CHAPTER 21: *Secret Keepers*

CHAPTER 22: *The Best Story Ever*

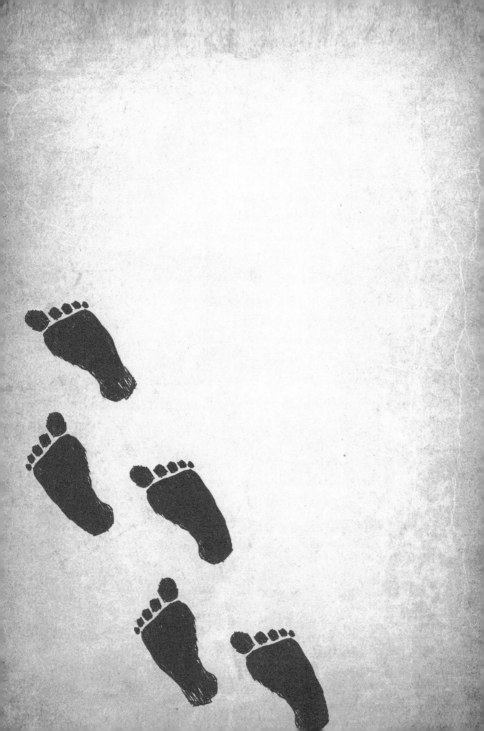

1

STORY BIRD

The weird shadow swept across the sky.

Ben blinked once, twice, three times, just in case an eyelash had drifted onto his eyeball. But it wasn't an eyelash. Something was moving between the clouds—something with an enormous wingspan and a long tail. Ben pressed his nose to the passenger window. "Grandpa? Did you see that?"

"So, you've got a voice after all," his grandfather said. "I was beginning to think you'd swallowed your tongue."

Benjamin Silverstein, age ten, had not swallowed his tongue. But it was true that he hadn't spoken since being picked up at the airport. He'd shrugged when his grandfather had asked, "How was your flight?" He'd nodded when his grandfather had asked, "Are you hungry?" He'd looked away when his grandfather had said, "I bet you miss your parents." But not a single word had come out of Ben. After a while, his grandfather had stopped talking, and they'd driven down the lonely two-lane highway in silence. There'd been nothing interesting to look at, no houses or gas stations or billboards. Just trees. Lots and lots of trees.

But then the shape had appeared, circling and swooping like a wind-kissed kite. "I've never seen a bird that big. It's got a tail like a rope."

Grandpa Abe slowed the car, then pulled to the side of the highway onto the gravel shoulder. "All right, already. Where is this bird?" he asked after the car came to a stop.

"It darted behind that cloud," Ben said. They

waited a few minutes, but the bird didn't reappear. The fluffy cloud drifted, revealing nothing but twilight sky.

"How big was it?"

Ben shrugged. "Big. Maybe as big as a helicopter."

"As big as a helicopter? And a tail like a rope?"

"Uh-huh."

"Hmmm. That doesn't sound right." Grandpa Abe scratched one of his overgrown gray eyebrows. "I've never seen a bird like that."

"Well, I saw it."

They waited another minute, but nothing flew out of the cloud. "Is the helicopter bird one of your *stories*?" Grandpa Abe's eyes narrowed with suspicion.

"What do you mean?"

"Your mother said you've been making up stories."

"I don't know what you're talking about," Ben grumbled. But he did know. That very morning, he'd made up a story that the pilot had called the house to cancel Ben's flight because he'd lost the keys to the plane. Then Ben had made up a story about losing his suitcase so he wouldn't have to go on this trip. Neither of those stories had worked. His parents had gone ahead with their plans and had sent Ben away.

Sometimes, Ben's stories worked to his advantage,

like the time he'd claimed that a California condor had snatched his math homework, when actually he'd forgotten to finish it. After his teacher pointed out that California condors don't usually do such things, Ben changed the bird to a pelican. Because pelicans are known troublemakers, the math teacher gave Ben an extra week to make up the assignment.

The way Ben saw it, stories were always more exciting than the truth.

Grandpa Abe sighed. "I should live so long to see a bird the size of a helicopter." He set his crinkled hands on the steering wheel and merged back onto the highway.

Ben sank into his seat and hugged his hamster cage to his chest. The hamster, a Chinese striped variety named Snooze, lay curled beneath a pile of chewed-up newspaper. The pile expanded and contracted with the hamster's deep, slumbering breaths. Ben wished at that very moment that he could be a hamster. Life would certainly

be easier if the entire world were a simple plastic rectangle. It didn't matter if the rectangle was set on a windowsill in Los Angeles or in the backseat of an old Cadillac driving down a highway in the middle of nowhere. The world inside the rectangle always stayed the same—stuff to chew, stuff to eat and drink, a wheel to waddle around in. No worries, no troubles, no changes.

"My grandson, the storyteller," Grandpa Abe mumbled.

"The bird wasn't a *story*," Ben said. "It was real."

2

WELCOME TO BUTTONVILLE

Here we are," Grandpa Abe announced as he exited the highway. The sign at the side of the road read:

Grandpa Abe drove down Main Street. The evening sky had darkened, but the corner streetlights shone brightly, casting their glow on the little town.

Ben frowned. It didn't look like the nicest town on Earth. It looked like the saddest town on Earth. There were no bright awnings, no corner fruit stands, no sidewalk tables where people sipped fancy drinks. Instead, many of the little shops that lined Main Street were empty, with signs in the windows:

"This town hasn't been the same since the button factory shut down," Grandpa Abe explained. "Most of the young families moved away to find work."

Ben had heard about the button factory. His mother kept a big bowl of buttons in the entertainment room back home in Los Angeles. "Those buttons were made by your grandfather," she'd told him. "He worked in a button factory most of his life."

"How come the factory shut down?" Ben asked, peering over the seat.

"Customers stopped wanting handmade buttons like these," Grandpa Abe replied, pointing to the big wooden buttons on the front of his shirt. "People should be so lucky to get handmade buttons. But it's cheaper to buy the plastic ones made by a machine."

Ben's gaze traveled up the wooden buttons and rested on his grandfather's wrinkled face. He hadn't seen his grandfather in six years. Ben's dad said it was because Grandpa Abe didn't like to travel. Because Ben had been only four years old at the time, he didn't remember anything about the

last visit. In the photos at home, Grandpa Abe had dark hair just like Ben and Ben's dad. But today, not a single hair remained on his shiny scalp.

Ben must have been staring pretty hard because his grandfather turned and winked at him. "You look different, too," Grandpa Abe said. "Your hair is shorter."

Ben ran his hand over his hair, which was cut to precisely three-quarters of an inch every two weeks. He thought about making up a story that his hair had been cut short because he'd been infested with Caribbean head lice, or because the ends had caught fire when he'd been struck by lightning. The real reason Ben had short hair was because his mother insisted it was *stylish*. She always took him to her hairdresser in Beverly Hills rather than to a barbershop, where the other boys went.

The Cadillac pulled up to a stop sign, just opposite a shop called the Dollar Store. A girl leaned out of the store's upstairs window. It wasn't her fuzzy pink bathrobe that caught Ben's attention, or the way her long blond hair glowed in the lamplight. What caught his attention was the way she was staring at the sky with her mouth wide open, as if seeing something very strange.

Ben unfastened his seat belt, rolled down the opposite window, and stuck his head out. Cool night air tickled his nose and ears. A shadow darted between two clouds—a shadow with enormous wings and a long, ropelike tail. If Ben had blinked, he would have missed it.

The girl looked down at Ben. Their eyes met. She'd seen it, too.

Then she mouthed a single word before disappearing behind the curtains.

"You want me to catch a cold?" Grandpa Abe complained.

As Ben closed the window and buckled his seat belt, Grandpa Abe drove through the intersection and turned onto a side street. Ben wrapped his arms around the hamster cage again. He wasn't an expert at reading lips, but he was pretty certain he knew what word the girl had said.

Dragon.

3

THE HOUSE ON PINE STREET

All the houses on Pine Street looked the same because they were company houses, built long ago by the owner of the button factory. Each was narrow with a white picket fence and three steps that led up to the front porch. Each was painted green with white trim and had a brick chimney. The only way to tell Grandpa Abe's house from the other houses was its cherry-red porch swing.

Grandpa Abe's cane tapped as he led Ben up the steps. The inside of his house smelled like coffee and onions, which wasn't so bad. Dust sparkled at the edges of a crowded bookshelf and a cluttered table. The furniture was patched and faded. Stuffing leaked from the sofa pillows. The entire house was the size of Ben's father's garage.

"Not much to look at, but it's home," Grandpa Abe said. "I know you're used to much better."

Ben set the hamster cage on the kitchen counter, right next to a bowl of peanuts, and looked around. There was no big-screen TV, no chandelier, no fancy Persian carpets. And clearly no housekeeper. Ben opened his hamster cage and dumped in two peanuts. They landed with soft *plop*s in the newspaper litter. As Snooze popped his head out of his nest and grabbed a treat, Ben wondered if his grandfather was poor.

Grandpa Abe rubbed

the back of his bald head. "Better go get your suitcase and I'll show you where you'll be sleeping."

Ben went back outside. A single star had appeared in the now cloudless sky. It never got very dark in Los Angeles because the city never went to sleep. But here in Buttonville, even with the lights glowing, night pressed in with eerie, charcoal-colored shadows. So dark. So quiet. Ben grabbed his suitcase and hurried back into the house.

"This is your bedroom," Grandpa Abe said as he opened the door behind the kitchen. He reached up and pulled a cord that hung from the ceiling. The light switched on, revealing a room not much bigger than a closet, with peeling yellow wallpaper and the faint odor of mothballs. "If I were you, I'd keep that mouse in here, out of Barnaby's reach."

"Snooze isn't a mouse; he's a hamster," Ben said as he dumped his suitcase onto the bed. Dust particles jumped off the quilt and took flight through the air like cosmic gymnasts. "Who's Barnaby?"

"Who's Barnaby? Barnaby's my cat."

"You have a cat?" Ben's heart thumped. He snatched the cage from the kitchen counter and hurried back into the bedroom. "A cat?"

"He's an excellent mouser, that cat," Grandpa Abe said proudly.

"Mouser?"

"What? You're surprised by that? Cats catch mice, that's what they do," Grandpa Abe said with a dismissive wave of his hand. "But Barnaby's never killed a hamster. As long as you keep the door closed, your hamster will be fine." Grandpa Abe pointed his cane around the room. "That's your closet and dresser drawers."

Ben set the cage on top of the dresser. His parents hadn't said anything about a cat that liked to hunt. But then again, his parents hadn't said anything about this trip except, "We need time alone to work out some troubles, so we're sending you to stay with your grandfather."

Grandpa Abe hobbled over and sat at the end of the bed. "So? What are your plans?"

"Plans?"

"For the summer. What do you want to do?"

Ben shrugged. "What is there to do?"

"There aren't any jobs, if that's what you were hoping for. Ever since the button factory closed, finding work is nearly impossible around here." Dust particles swirled beneath the overhead bulb. "You could come with me to the senior center. We've got bingo on Monday, board games on Tuesday, dance lessons on Wednesday, guest lectures on Thursday, and Friday is birthday day, when we celebrate all the birthdays for that week. Saturday is pudding day."

"Pudding day?"

"We eat pudding. It's fun."

Ben didn't want to hurt his grandfather's feelings, so he simply said, "Yeah, sounds like fun."

Grandpa Abe reached over and patted Ben's

knee. "Cheer up, boychik. It won't be that bad. You'll find something to do. Boys always find something to do. You'll keep yourself busy while your parents work out their troubles, and then you'll be back home for school before you know it." With a grunt and some creaking of the knees, he got to his feet. "In the meantime, I have a leftover brisket that I'll warm in the microwave."

As soon as his grandfather had left the room, Ben released a groan that he'd been holding since he got off the plane. This was going to be the worst summer ever. Summer was supposed to be spent swimming in his pool with friends or rowing at the lake. Not stuck at the senior center playing board games and eating pudding.

"Nothing fancy around here," Grandpa Abe explained fifteen minutes later as they sat at the kitchen table. He handed Ben a chipped plate and a fork with a bent handle. "Been living the bachelor life for twenty years. Don't care much for fancy. I need fancy like I need a hole in the head."

Dinner was pretty good. The potatoes were creamy and the brisket wasn't too dry. The pickles were served right out of the jar, and the soda was sipped straight from the can. "No need for glasses," Grandpa Abe explained. "Glasses need to be washed, and I don't like doing dishes." He nodded toward the stack of dirty dishes that towered in the sink.

Grandpa Abe didn't seem to care about manners. He chewed loudly, scraping the last bits of food right off his plate and into his mouth. After a loud burp, he wiped his mouth on his sleeve. Ben looked around. Napkins didn't appear to be a part of Grandpa Abe's world, so Ben wiped his mouth on his sleeve, too.

"Let's go sit on the porch and count the stars," Grandpa Abe said as he reached for his cane. "And maybe we'll catch a glimpse of that bird, the one as big as a helicopter." He winked at Ben, clearly still believing that the bird had come from Ben's imagination.

As Ben carried his plate to the sink, he pictured the blond girl. *Dragon*, she'd mouthed. Ben frowned.

He didn't think for an instant that the rope-tailed bird was actually a dragon. Dragons weren't real. Dragons were stories. And he knew all about stories.

But the bird was something, and if not a dragon, then what?

4

DOLLAR STORE GIRL

Grab some breakfast," Grandpa Abe said the next morning as he pointed to a box of dough-nuts. "We've got errands to run."

Doughnuts for breakfast? Back home, Ben always had oatmeal with bananas or whole-grain cereal. "Thanks." He took a powdered-sugar bite.

"You'd better keep your bedroom door shut. Barnaby's on the prowl."

Ben hadn't yet seen Barnaby the cat, but he'd imagined him to be a gigantic killer with fangs and glowing red eyes. He checked on Snooze, who was asleep as usual. Then he shut the bedroom door and followed his grandfather out to the car.

Although Ben still didn't want to spend an entire summer in Buttonville, he decided, as he munched on the doughnut, that things weren't all that bad. His grandfather hadn't made him take a shower that morning and hadn't asked a bunch of questions like, "Did you brush *and* floss? Did you put on *clean* socks? Did you take your vitamins?" Since Grandpa Abe was wearing the same clothes he'd worn when he'd picked Ben up at the airport, Ben decided to wear yesterday's clothes, too. He never got to do that at home.

But to Ben's disappointment, Buttonville's Main Street looked just as threadbare in the daylight as it had the night before—maybe worse because now all the flaking paint, broken windows, and cracked sidewalks could be seen. A pair of old men sat on a bench outside the Buttonville Hardware Store. They waved as Grandpa Abe drove past. Grandpa Abe waved back. A woman washing the windows of the Buttonville Diner also waved. Grandpa Abe waved back. The girl with the long blond hair who'd been leaning out the window last night was now standing outside the Dollar Store, a broom in her hand. She didn't wave, but she watched intently as Grandpa Abe parked the car.

"So? What will you want for dinner?" Grandpa Abe asked, pulling a canvas hat out of the glove compartment and setting it on his bald head. "How about a nice brisket? You like a nice brisket? They make a nice ready-to-eat brisket at the market."

Ben didn't point out that they'd had brisket the night before. He was watching the girl across

the street, and she appeared to be watching him.

"Did you swallow your tongue again?" Grandpa Abe asked.

"Sorry," Ben said. "Sure, I like brisket."

"Then brisket it is." Clutching his cane, Grandpa Abe struggled out of the car. Ben hurried around to the driver's side to help him. "Looks like Pearl Petal is coming this way," Grandpa Abe said with a slight nod of his head. The blond girl was crossing the street, still clutching the broom. "She's a nice girl, that Pearl, but a bit of a troublemaker. Watch yourself." The tip of his wooden cane tapped against the sidewalk as Grandpa Abe headed into the Food 4 Less Market.

Pearl was fast. She was like one of those professional speed-walkers, the way she swung her arms, the heels of her sneakers barely touching the ground, the hem of her green Dollar Store apron flapping against her knees.

"What do you think that thing was?" she asked after she'd come to a halt directly in front of Ben. A big, wide gap sat between her two front teeth. Her

cheeks were pinkish and her eyes bright green. She leaned so close he could smell her cherry lip balm.

"Uh…" Ben paused. Then he stepped back. Did this girl know anything about personal space? "What thing?" He knew perfectly well *what thing*, but he didn't know what else to say.

She straightened, which made her a whole head taller than Ben. "That thing, last night in the sky. What do you think it was?"

It sure looked like a dragon, he thought. But he didn't say that out loud. "Maybe it was a bird?"

"A bird?" She screwed up her face. "But it was huge, and it had a long tail. You really think that thing was a bird? Don't you think it looked like a dragon?"

"Dragons aren't real."

She shrugged. "Maybe they are, maybe they aren't. Hey, what's your name?"

"Ben Silverstein."

"I'm Pearl Petal. What are you doing in Button-ville, Ben Silverstein?"

"I'm visiting my grandfather for the summer."

"The whole summer? Your parents sent you to this boring town for the whole summer? Are they mad at you or something?"

Ben chewed on his lower lip as he thought about making up a story. He could tell Pearl that his parents had sent him to Buttonville because they were secret agents and they had to go on a dangerous mission. Or he could tell her that his parents were astronauts and they were headed to Mars for the summer. There were lots of stories that were more interesting than the truth—that his parents were having troubles and arguing all the time. Ben didn't want to tell anyone the truth, especially not a girl he barely knew.

"You sure wear fancy clothes," Pearl said. "I get most of my clothes from the Dollar Store. These shorts only cost a dollar." She pointed to her shiny red basketball shorts, which hung below her knees. Ben didn't know how much his brand-new jeans had cost, but his mom had ordered them from a catalog. "Do you have any brothers or sisters?"

"No," Ben replied.

"Me neither. It's just me and my mom and dad. But my great-aunt Gladys, who has trouble remembering things, lives in our basement. She smells like menthol cough drops. Most of the people around here are old like Aunt Gladys. That's because a lot of families moved away so they could find jobs, and they took their kids with them." She took a quick breath. "There's this one girl who still lives here named Victoria, but stay away from her because she can't keep a secret. Believe me, I learned the hard way. I told Victoria that I'd found a nest of baby raccoons under my house and that I was feeding them table scraps, and Victoria told my mom and I got into huge trouble."

This girl sure likes to talk. "I need to go help my grandfather. He's in the store." Ben tried to walk away, but Pearl stepped in front of him.

"You really think it was a bird?" she asked, lowering her voice. She leaned on the broom and stared at him.

No, he did not think it was a bird. Ben Silverstein was no dummy. He knew what he'd seen. But never in a million years would he admit it. That would be like admitting he'd seen the tooth fairy.

"I saw it before," Pearl said. "Last week I saw it land on the roof of the old button factory. I think it lives there." Then she smiled. "I'm going to investigate later. Wanna join me?"

Grandpa Abe's words replayed in Ben's head. *She's a nice girl, that Pearl, but a bit of a trouble-maker. Watch yourself.* Ben didn't want trouble. He wanted to go home.

"I can't go," Ben told her. "I need to help my grandfather...make brisket."

Pearl frowned. "What are you going to do after you make brisket?"

"Eat it."

"And then what?"

Ben shrugged. "I'll do *something*."

"Well, just so you know, there's *nothing* to do in this boring town." She pulled a stick of gum from her apron pocket and began to chew. She offered him a stick of gum, but he politely shook his head. "The bowling alley closed, and the movie theater only shows movies on Friday night. We don't even have a swimming pool, unless you count the plastic pool over at the senior center, but it's no fun because the seniors yell at you if you splash."

No swimming pool? Back home, Ben had a pool in his backyard. All his friends had pools in their backyards.

"Well, if you change your mind"—she pointed to the embroidered words on her apron: **YOU GET MORE AT THE DOLLAR STORE**—"my family lives above the store. If you see any more *birds*, let me know." She swept a white button into the street drain, then headed back across the intersection.

If the town was as boring as Pearl said, this was going to be a long, uneventful summer.

5

JELLY BEAN MAN

The Food 4 Less Market was tiny compared with the grocery store back home. Just five aisles and only one cashier. There was no barista making cappuccinos, no fancy bottles of water from Fiji. The grocery bags were plastic, not canvas, and the day's special was bologna, not goose-liver pâté.

Ben's grandfather stood second in line for the cash register. He'd crammed a lot of groceries into his cart. There were kosher hot dogs, white bread, and mustard. There were frozen pizzas and egg rolls, bagels and cream cheese, a box of Sugar Loops, and two boxes of doughnuts. Ben smiled. No fruits or vegetables or stuff that was "healthy."

"Hello, madame," the man at the front of the line said to the cashier. He wore a long black raincoat, which seemed odd, since the day was warm and sunny. "I wish to purchase this can of fish broth, this can of condensed milk, and some kiwi-flavored jelly beans."

The cashier, a girl with a pimple-covered nose, tapped her fingernails on the counter. "We don't have kiwi-flavored jelly beans."

"Then could you be so kind as to special-order them for me?" the man asked. "I need them as soon as possible." He pushed his long red hair behind his shoulders.

The cashier took a piece of paper from a drawer. "How many do you want?" she asked.

"Two thousand boxes."

"Two thousand boxes?" Ben blurted.

"That's a lot of jelly beans," Grandpa Abe said

as he leaned on the handle of the grocery cart. "You'll rot your teeth eating that much candy."

The man slowly turned to face Ben and his grandfather. His red mustache was waxed so that it stuck out in individual strands. The mustache quivered as the man spoke, reminding Ben of a cat's whiskers. "I appreciate your concern for my dental health, but there is no need to worry. I am not fond of kiwi-flavored jelly beans. I eat only meat."

"Only meat?" Grandpa Abe asked. "What about a knish? You like a good knish?"

The man's irises, which were shaped like black half-moons, suddenly swelled. His nose, which was upturned, started to twitch. He sniffed, and his gaze darted to Ben. "Are you the owner of a Chinese striped hamster?"

"Yes," Ben said with surprise. "How did you know?"

With very sharp nails, the man plucked a little hair from Ben's shirt. "The Chinese striped has a unique odor, quite different from the standard hamster." He brought the hair to his nose, which twitched faster, as if powered by a little motor. "This one is male. Young. Tender. Delicious with pepper." He licked his lips.

Delicious with pepper? An eerie shiver trickled down Ben's spine. He'd never heard of anyone eating a hamster. Who would do a thing like that?

"You must be new around here," Grandpa Abe said to the man. "Where are you from?"

The man straightened. His nose stopped twitching. "I'm from...far away."

"Two thousand boxes will cost a lot of money," the cashier said. "You sure you want to order that many?"

"Money is of no concern." The man reached into a trouser pocket and pulled out a wad of cash, which he set on the counter. Because Grandpa Abe and the cashier were staring openmouthed at the cash, they didn't notice the little piece of paper that drifted from the man's pocket and landed at Ben's feet. "My employer would like the boxes delivered as soon as they arrive."

"Who do you work for?" the cashier asked as she picked up the wad of cash.

"I am employed by the brilliant and talented Dr. Woo." The man tapped his polished shoe. "As a matter of fact, if we could conclude our business, I need to get back to work. I am Dr. Woo's assistant."

"Buttonville has a new doctor?" Grandpa Abe asked. "What kind of doctor?"

"A worm doctor," the man replied. "Dr. Woo is renowned worldwide for her work with worms. She tends to their illnesses and needs." Grandpa Abe and the cashier shared a confused look. "Do you have a pen, dear woman, so that I can fill out the order form?" The cashier handed the red-haired man a pen. While he filled out the order form, Ben reached down and grabbed the piece of paper. It was a recipe card.

RECIPE FOR ARTIFICIAL DRAGON'S MILK
USING KNOWN WORLD INGREDIENTS

- ONE CAN OF FISH BROTH
- ONE CAN OF CONDENSED MILK

1. MIX TOGETHER.
2. HEAT UNTIL THE LIQUID COMES TO A BOIL.
3. SERVE PIPING HOT.

Ben read it again. Was this for real?

The man finished filling out the order form, then handed it to the cashier. She read it.

"It says here you want the jelly beans delivered to the old button factory, but the button factory is closed."

"Dr. Woo is renting the old factory. It will house her worm hospital." Then the man collected his grocery bag, which contained the can of fish broth and the can of condensed milk. After a quick bow to the cashier, he strode toward the exit. Ben hurried after him.

"Excuse me," Ben called.

The man turned on his heels. "Yes?"

"You dropped this." Ben handed him the recipe card.

The man's whiskers twitched as he took the card. "Thank you," he said.

"That's a weird recipe," Ben said. "Is it for the worms? At the worm hospital?" He didn't know anything about worms, except that if you cut them in half, they still wiggled.

"The recipe is not for worms," the man replied. "Worms do not drink dragon's milk. Only dragons drink dragon's milk." He offered no further explanation. He bowed again, then left.

"Did I hear that man say something about dragons?" Grandpa Abe asked when Ben returned to the counter.

"Uh-huh," Ben said.

"Oy gevalt." Grandpa Abe shook his head, then began to stack his groceries on the counter. "Just what we need. Another crazy person in Buttonville."

6

SEA HORSE FACE

While Grandpa Abe rattled around in the kitchen, Ben fed a piece of doughnut to Snooze the hamster. Then he opened the bedroom window. There was no screen, so he stuck out his head. It was late morning, and the sun streamed between his grandfather's house and the house next door. A little path was worn into the side yard between the houses.

"Today is Friday," Grandpa Abe called. "Birthday day at the senior center." Ben leaned on the windowsill. Going to the senior center didn't sound like much fun. He could tell his grandfather that he had a stomachache. Or maybe he'd make up a better story—that he had a medical condition that made him allergic to other people's birthday cakes.

Then again, eating frosting might be better than hanging around the house, wondering what his friends back home were doing. Wondering if his parents were going to stay together. Wondering about that giant *bird*.

"Merooow."

A large black cat turned into the side yard and pranced up the path. His tail stuck straight up, and something swung from his mouth. The cat stopped beneath the window and stared up at Ben, his yellow eyes widening with surprise. He wiggled his bottom.

"Oh no," Ben said, "you're not coming in here." But before he could close the window, the cat leaped onto the sill, then jumped onto the bed. Ben threw himself at the dresser, standing between the cat and the hamster cage. "Don't even think about it," he warned. "Go on. Shoo." Ben waved his hands toward the open bedroom door. "Shoo!"

But the cat didn't shoo. His pitiful victim dangled from his smiling mouth. Snooze the hamster stopped eating the doughnut and scurried into his nest. The rustling sound caught the cat's attention.

"Grandpa, can you please call your cat?" Ben hollered.

"Here, Barnaby, Barnaby, Barnaby. Come get some yum-yums."

The sound of a can opener was apparently more interesting than a hamster's rustling. With a leap, Barnaby soared through the air like a trapeze artist, landed gracefully in the doorway, then pranced into the kitchen. With a sigh of relief, Ben hurriedly shut the door. "And stay out," he grumbled.

He was about to tell Snooze that he wouldn't

let that bad kitty back into the bedroom when something squeaked.

Ben leaned over his bed. There, in the middle of the quilt, lay Barnaby's victim. Only it wasn't dead. It wiggled and squeaked again.

And then it shot a fountain of flame right at Ben's face. "Whoa!" Ben cried, ducking as the flame whooshed over his head.

As suddenly as the flame had appeared, it disappeared. Ben felt his face and hair to make sure nothing was on fire. Then a second flame shot upward, but this time, it reached only a few feet off the bed. The flame disappeared, and the creature squeaked again.

A third flame emerged, but it was weak, like a sparkler on the Fourth of July. It fizzled and popped, extinguishing with a hissing sound. The little creature coughed.

What just happened? How did...? How could...? Ben's legs trembled.

After a minute or two had passed and no

more flames appeared, Ben knelt beside the
bed. He wasn't about to touch it, whatever *it*
was. The creature's body and wings were black,
but one of the wings was torn. Was it a bat? Ben
had seen photos of bats, so he knew they had
all sorts of weird faces. Some looked like foxes,
some like mice. There were dog-faced bats and
monkey-faced bats. This one had a long snout,
like a sea horse.

He leaned closer and discovered a problem with

his bat theory. Bats were mammals and covered with fur. This thing was covered with glossy scales.

And of course, bats didn't spout fire. As far as Ben knew, no animals spouted fire. No *real* animals.

"Ben? Your mother's on the phone." Grandpa Abe rapped on the door. "Be a good boy and come talk to your mother."

"Okay." Ben didn't want to leave the creature, which coughed again and looked up at him with half-closed eyes. "I'll be right back," he whispered. He closed the bedroom window so the killer cat couldn't sneak back in, and he made sure to close the bedroom door, too. He didn't mention the bat to his grandfather, who was putting away groceries. "You can't keep a fire-breathing bat," he'd surely say. "It's too dangerous. It'll burn your ears off."

No need to tell him just yet. A fire-breathing bat was a pretty cool thing to find, and Ben wanted to spend a bit more time with it before he turned it over to an adult.

"Hello?" Ben said as he picked up the phone

receiver. The phone was one of the old-fashioned kind that attached to the wall.

"Hi, Benjamin," his mother chirped. "I just wanted to see how things were going. Is your grandfather feeding you?"

"Yes."

"Good. Be sure to help him carry things. And be sure to help him with the chores around the house. He's getting old. And be sure to keep your room clean, and be sure to brush your teeth, and be sure to..." She paused. "Oh, just have fun. I want you to have lots and lots of fun."

"I will," Ben said, his gaze fixed on his bedroom door.

"You're not still mad that we sent you there, are you?" Silence filled the line.

If asked that question five minutes ago, Ben would have told his mother that yes, he was really mad that she'd sent him to stay in a boring town in the middle of nowhere with a grandfather he barely knew. But with a fire-breathing bat lying on his bed—well, that changed everything.

"I'm not mad," Ben said. Barnaby the cat pawed at the bedroom door. Then he pressed his barrel-shaped body against the wood, a low growl vibrating as he pushed, trying to get in. "Uh, I gotta go, but don't worry so much, Mom. I'm fine."

"Okay, sweetie. Your father and I just want you to know that we love you."

"I love you, too. Bye." Ben hung up. "Shoo," he said waving his hands. "Shoo." The cat flicked his tail, then moseyed over to his water bowl. Ben cracked open the door and peered into the bedroom. The little creature lay in the exact same spot on the bed, licking its injured wing.

"Grandpa Abe, are there any animal doctors in Buttonville?"

"Apparently, we have a worm doctor," Grandpa Abe said as he set a bag of potato chips in the cupboard. "This we need? A worm doctor?"

"Yeah, but are there any other doctors? You

know"—Ben searched his brain for the word—"a veterinarian?" He tried to keep his voice from trembling with excitement. "Just in case my hamster gets sick or something like that. Not for any other reason."

Grandpa Abe shook his head. "We should be so lucky to have a veterinarian in Buttonville. The nearest one's a four-hour drive. Took Barnaby there a few months back when he got a bellyache from eating too many mice. That cat loves mice."

Barnaby wound between Ben's ankles, rubbing his cheeks against Ben's jeans. "I'm going to finish unpacking," Ben told his grandfather. He didn't want to seem rude, so he added, "And I'm going to keep the door closed so Barnaby doesn't get in and eat my hamster."

"Okay by me," Grandpa Abe said. He leaned across the counter and turned on the radio. Music from days gone by filled the kitchen. Grandpa Abe tapped his foot and hummed along to the swinging rhythm.

With the bedroom door shut tight, Ben knelt

beside the bed. The creature's eyes were closed; its little chest rose and fell in quick breaths. A wheezy sound came out of its snout. Ben frowned. The nearest veterinarian was four hours away. Grandpa Abe would have to drive there, but that would mean telling him about the fire-breathing bat.

The little creature suddenly rolled over. Was that a tail? Ben reached out cautiously, smoothing the quilt so he could get a better look. It *was* a tail. A long, barbed tail. He sat back on his heels, a huge grin spreading across his face. His whole body tingled.

Bats didn't have barbed tails. Bats didn't have scales. Bats didn't breathe fire.

As impossible as it seemed, Ben knew what lay on his bed.

7

PEARL'S PROMISE

I'm going to take a nap," Grandpa Abe announced as he patted his belly. He grabbed his cane and shuffled across the crumb-coated kitchen floor. Ben had eaten a bologna sandwich and a pickle for lunch, but he didn't remember chewing or tasting them. He'd been thinking about the baby dragon that was lying on his bed. How long could it survive without help?

The red-haired man with the dragon's milk recipe had said he worked at the old button factory.

A person with a dragon's milk recipe might be a person who knows a thing or two about dragons. "Grandpa?"

"Hmmm?" Grandpa Abe settled on the patched couch. He stretched out his long, skinny legs and rested his head on a moth-nibbled pillow.

"Can I go for a walk?"

"Can you go for a walk? Of course you can go for a walk."

"Thanks." Back home, Ben wasn't allowed to go on walks alone. Too much traffic, too many strangers. Plus, everything was so spread out in Los Angeles, it could take an hour just to get to the mall. But if Ben stood on Main Street in Buttonville, he could see from one end of town to the other. There was no way he'd get lost.

As Ben added his lunch plate to the pile in the sink, he remembered that he'd promised his mother to help with the chores. "I'll wash these when I get back," he said.

"Okay by me." Grandpa Abe closed his eyes.

"I'll be heading to the senior center later. There's an extra key to the house under the welcome mat, just in case I'm not here when you get back." He rolled onto his side.

"Okay."

Ben found a cookie tin on the kitchen counter. He shook out the crumbs, then set folded sheets of paper towels inside. After grabbing a rusty spatula, he hurried into his room.

The creature lay on the quilt, its eyes still closed. Ben slid the spatula under the creature, gently lifted it, and set it on the bed of paper towels. For a moment, he worried about the flammability of the paper. But no sparks shot out of the creature's snout. "Don't be scared," he whispered. He put the lid on the tin, then carried it into the living room.

Snores streamed out of Grandpa Abe's half-open mouth. Barnaby perched on Grandpa's chest, leisurely cleaning his front paws. He seemed to have forgotten about the wounded creature he'd abandoned on Ben's bed, and he paid no attention as Ben tiptoed past and out the front door. Ben glanced back, just to make sure his bedroom door was closed tight.

Gripping the cookie tin, Ben set off down the sidewalk. Town Hall loomed in the distance, guiding the way back to Main Street. In just a few minutes, Ben stood in front of the Dollar Store.

He barely knew Pearl Petal, but he needed her help. Even though Grandpa Abe had called Pearl a troublemaker, Ben felt he could trust her. After all, they'd both seen the giant bird and she'd mouthed the word *dragon*. She'd told him that the giant bird lived on the roof of the old button factory. And she'd said she was going to investigate. If she took him to the factory, maybe they'd find the red-haired man who'd said he worked there. Ben hoped she hadn't left already.

The Dollar Store's front window was stacked with all sorts of stuff you could buy for a dollar: baskets, beach balls, bags of tortilla chips, and brooms. Voices drifted from the open window above the store. Glasses and silverware clinked.

"Hello?" Ben called. A head of blond hair poked out the window.

"Hey, it's you." Pearl looked down at him. "What's that you're carrying?"

Ben put the cookie tin behind his back. "Are you still going to the old button factory? To find that… *bird*?"

"Yeah, as soon as I finish lunch." She smiled. "You want to go with me?"

"Yes, because…" Ben tapped his feet, then looked around. The sidewalk was empty. The nearest pair of ears belonged to a woman who was walking her dog across the street. "I found something," he told Pearl.

Pearl disappeared. A few moments later, the OPEN sign rattled as she burst out the front door. "What did you find?" she asked, her eyes wide with expectation. A checkered napkin was tucked into her T-shirt.

Ben narrowed his eyes. "You have to promise not to tell anyone."

"Yeah, okay. I promise," she said, holding up her hand as if swearing an oath.

"Because if you tell your mom or your dad, they might take it away."

"I said I promise. I always keep my promises."

Ben lowered his voice. Then he slowly slid the tin out from behind his back. "Remember how you said that the bird looked like a dragon?"

Pearl nodded. Her eyes got so big they looked like they might pop right off her face. "Did you find dragon poop?"

"No. Something better."

Very carefully, so as not to startle the creature, Ben pulled off the lid.

"Is that a toy?" Pearl asked as she leaned closer. Then she inhaled so long and hard that if any bugs had been flying around, they surely would have been sucked into her mouth right between the big gap in her teeth. "Whoa! It's breathing!" She reached out to touch the creature, but Ben pulled the tin away.

"Be careful. It shoots fire," he explained. "Grandpa's cat caught it. Its wing is torn."

"Ben? Do you know what you've found?" Pearl's green eyes sparkled as if they'd been dipped in glitter. "Do you?"

Ben swallowed hard. When he spoke, his voice was a bit shaky. "I think it's a baby dragon."

"It sure is." Pearl smiled. "Do you think it belongs to the big dragon?"

"Maybe."

"Then we have to get it back to its mother. We have to go to the button factory."

Ben didn't want to return the baby to its mother. He wanted to keep it. But he didn't know how to take care of it.

"I've lived here all my life, and suddenly we have dragons in Buttonville. This is amazing." Pearl looked over her shoulder. "Better put the lid back on so no one else sees it." Ben did, and just in time, because a woman with hair as yellow as Pearl's stuck her head out the upstairs window.

"Pearl? What are you doing?"

"Hi, Mom. I'm talking to my new friend, Ben."

Mrs. Petal smiled. She had a big gap between her front teeth, too. "Hello, Ben. You must be Abe's grandson. We've heard a lot about you."

"Hello," Ben said.

"I bet it's exciting to live in Los Angeles. This town must seem very boring to you."

Ben shrugged. "Well..."

"Mom, can I go for a walk with Ben?"

Mrs. Petal pursed her lips and thought for a moment. "I guess so. But you still have chores, so be back before we close."

"Okay," Pearl answered. She yanked the napkin out of her collar and tossed it into the Dollar Store. Then she grabbed Ben's arm and pulled him down the sidewalk.

"Don't get into trouble," Mrs. Petal called. "*Please* don't get into trouble."

"I won't," Pearl called back. Then she grumbled, "Everyone always thinks I'm going to get into trouble."

The scent of french fries and grilled burgers

drifted out the door of the Buttonville Diner as the kids passed by. "Maybe the baby dragon fell out of the big dragon's nest," Pearl said as they hurried down Main Street. "Then your grandpa's cat found it."

"Maybe," Ben said, though the baby seemed very small to have come from the humongous creature that had flown between the clouds.

Pearl led the way, turning onto Fir Street. Her shiny red basketball shorts swished with her hurried steps. They cut through a church parking lot and darted around the back of an abandoned gas station. Pearl's stride was longer than Ben's, her steps faster. He had to jog to keep up.

"If the nest is on the button factory roof, like I think it is, then we'll have to climb up so we can give the baby dragon back," Pearl said as they crossed over to Maple Street.

Ben stopped walking. There were many things he dreamed of doing. Getting past level thirty-six in *Galaxy Games* was one of those things. Learning how to ride a skateboard was another one of those things. But facing an enormous mother dragon—

not one of those things. The wall of flame the mother dragon could shoot from her snout would be a million times bigger than the one that had come out of her baby. "Uh, Pearl, I don't think we should climb to the roof. I have a better idea."

"A better idea?" She skidded to a stop. "I'm listening."

He told her about the red-haired man who worked at the button factory.

"That's impossible," she said, pushing blond wisps from her face. "No one works at the button factory. It closed years ago."

"The man had a recipe in his pocket for artificial dragon's milk. And he bought the stuff to make it."

Ben expected Pearl to laugh. He expected her to give him a playful shove and say something like, "No way! That's crazy." But she didn't. She twirled a lock of her hair, her eyes glazing over as she went into a deep thinking place.

"Pearl? Did you hear what I said?"

"Dragon's milk," she mumbled. "Then he must know about the big dragon." She suddenly spun

around. "Woo-hoo!" she cried. A squirrel that had been sitting on a garbage can skittered away. *"Woo-hoo!"* Pearl spun again. "This is amazing. Isn't this amazing? Don't you think this is amazing?"

Ben broke into a huge grin. "Yes, it's amazing."

But the mood was broken by a sickly sound—something between a squeak and a cough—that came from inside the tin. Ben opened the lid, and he and Pearl peered inside. A little green stain had spread across the paper towels. "Do you think that green stuff is blood?" Pearl asked.

"Maybe," Ben said. "The stupid cat must have stabbed the dragon with one of his sharp teeth."

"We'd better hurry."

8

THE OLD BUTTON FACTORY

The factory stood at the very edge of town. A wrought-iron fence surrounded the property. The entry gate was closed with a padlock. A sign hung on the gate.

WELCOME TO DR. WOO'S WORM HOSPITAL.
DR. WOO DOES NOT TREAT CATS, DOGS, PIGS, RATS, SNAKES, TURTLES, FISH, FROGS, OR ANY OTHER CREATURE THAT IS NOT A WORM.
DR. WOO SEES WORMS BY APPOINTMENT ONLY.
IF YOU DON'T HAVE AN APPOINTMENT,

→KEEP OUT!←

"We don't have an appointment," Ben said with a sigh.

"And we don't have a worm," Pearl said. "But somebody in there knows something about dragons or else they wouldn't be making dragon's milk." Without another word, she climbed right over the gate. Even though Ben would normally pay attention to a sign, he knew that without help, the little dragon might not survive. So, standing on tiptoe, he carefully handed the cookie tin through the bars into Pearl's hands. Then he scrambled over. When his feet touched down on the other side, he expected an alarm to ring or police sirens to sound. Or someone to holler, "You kids are trespassing!" But the afternoon was quiet. No traffic hum, no car alarms, no helicopters.

"How come it's so quiet?" Ben asked.

"It's always this quiet."

"Thanks for holding the dragon," Ben said as he took back the cookie tin. He peeked inside. The creature lay in the same position, its small, scaly

chest moving with shallow breaths. "The green stain's the same."

"Good," Pearl said. "Maybe that means it stopped bleeding."

A long driveway led from the gate. An overgrown lawn spread out on either side. Sparks of color caught Ben's eyes. He reached down and picked up a red wooden button. Then a green one.

"You can find buttons all over Buttonville," Pearl explained. "The pigeons collect them and put them in their nests."

The driveway ended at a rectangular concrete building that looked like a fortress belonging to a mad scientist. The windows on all ten floors were dark. Many were broken. As the kids neared the old factory, a sudden wind rushed in, rustling Pearl's hair and howling through the broken panes.

"It sounds like the place is haunted," Ben said.

"Maybe it is." Pearl pointed up at the roof. "That corner is where the dragon landed. Can you see anything?"

"No. But if a dragon built a nest on top of this old factory, it's probably in the center of the roof, where no one can see it."

"That makes sense," Pearl said. Then she led Ben around to the side of the building. "Look." She pointed to a metal ladder that ran up to the roof. "It's a fire-escape ladder. We can climb to the top."

"I don't want to climb to the top," Ben said. The ladder was rusty, and when Pearl grabbed it, it jiggled. While he was worried about the ladder coming loose, he was more worried about what might be hanging out on the roof. "What if the mother dragon is sleeping and we wake her up?" The wind picked up and a loud howl sounded. Pearl let go of the ladder.

"We have to give the baby back to its mother," she said.

"No, we don't," Ben said. "I've been thinking about it. Dragons are reptiles, right?"

Pearl shrugged. "I guess so."

"Well, reptiles don't stay with their parents. Right after hatching, a baby snake slithers away.

A baby turtle swims away. They don't need a mom or a dad. So maybe baby dragons are the same." Ben clutched the cookie tin. "If the baby dragon doesn't need its mother, then I want to keep it."

Something growled.

Pearl glanced around nervously. "Okay. But it still needs to see a doctor. Let's try knocking on the front door."

A note was taped to the front door.

THE WORM HOSPITAL IS **CLOSED** UNTIL IT IS **OPEN**.

Pearl knocked. Then she knocked harder. "Hello?" she called.

A light turned on inside. It trickled through the crack beneath the door. Pearl stepped back and grabbed Ben's arm as footsteps sounded. "Someone's coming," she whispered.

A dead bolt released with a loud *click*, and the door creaked as it opened. The red-haired man stood in the doorway. "Yes?" he asked, his red eyebrows raised expectantly. He no longer wore the black raincoat. His white shirtsleeves were rolled up, exposing arms that could only be described as *furry*. A red vest and a pair of perfectly pressed black trousers made him look a bit like a waiter in a fancy restaurant. He held an empty birdcage.

"Uh, hi," Ben said. "I saw you in the grocery store when you were ordering all those jelly beans."

"Kiwi-flavored jelly beans," the man said, the birdcage dangling from his fingers. That's when Ben noticed a small pile at the bottom of the cage. It looked like ashes. "Are you the delivery boy?"

"No," Ben said. "Don't you remember me? You picked a hamster hair off my shirt. And I found your recipe for dragon's milk and gave it back to you."

The man smacked his lips. "Ah, yes, I remember.

A Chinese striped hamster." *Delicious with pepper.* "If you are not the delivery boy, then why are you here?"

"We need your help," Pearl said.

"Dr. Woo's Worm Hospital is closed."

"It's a big emergency," Ben said.

"Yes, an emergency."

"Do you have a sick worm?" the man asked.

"No," Ben said, holding out the cookie tin. "But I found something. And it's hurt."

The red-haired man's whiskers twitched. His irises dilated as he sniffed the air. "Do I detect a wyvern?" He pressed his nose against the tin. "Yes, indeed! My dear boy, you have found our missing hatchling."

"Hatchling?" Ben realized that the man must be talking about the baby dragon. "Do you know how to take care of...hatchlings?"

"Dr. Woo knows how to take care of most everything." The red-haired man shifted the birdcage to his left hand, then held out his right hand. "I'll take it. You can leave it with me."

"I don't want to leave it with you," Ben said. "I'd like to keep it. I just need Dr. Woo to fix it."

"Keep it?" The man frowned. "That is not possible." Then his gaze darted to the birdcage. The little pile of ashes began to glow, sparks rising as if it were the remains of a very tiny campfire. "The phoenix arises. Wait here." He shut the door.

"Phoenix?" Pearl said. "I know what that is. I know all about birds. I have a bird-nest collection." Then she went on to explain: "A phoenix is a bird that bursts into flame, then is reborn from its ashes."

Before Ben could comment, the door opened and the red-haired man, now empty-handed, stood once again in the doorway. "Are you from the Imaginary World?" he asked the kids.

Ben and Pearl shared a bewildered look. Then they both shook their heads.

"Then you cannot keep the hatchling. Imaginary World creatures are not allowed to live in the Known World. It is against the rules."

Known World? Imaginary World? A shiver

slithered down Ben's spine. What was this man talking about?

"When you say the 'Imaginary World,' do you mean it's an actual place?" Pearl asked.

"Of course it is an actual place," the man replied. "Where else would the hatchling have come from?" Then he cleared his throat. "Oh dear, perhaps I should not have said that."

A faint squeak echoed inside the cookie tin. Although Ben's head was swimming with questions, he knew the baby dragon needed help. "Please, could we see Dr. Woo?"

"Dr. Woo is not here. She is making a house call. But I am in charge during her absence." The man stepped aside. "If you will not relinquish the creature, then you had best come in."

9

MR. TABBY

They stood in a big, cold room. Sparkling cobwebs crisscrossed the high ceiling. Strips of peeling white paint hung from the walls as if something very large had been sharpening its claws in the concrete. A faded sign stood on its side against the far wall next to an elevator. Two doors flanked the room.

"Please forgive the mess," the man said. "We have only been here

BUTTONVILLE
BUTTON FACTORY

a few days. It is rather difficult to move an entire hospital." He nodded toward some moving boxes that were stacked in one corner. A pile of buttons lay in another corner, next to a broom. The birdcage was nowhere to be seen.

"How come you need such a big place?" Ben asked. "Worms are so small."

"We have one room for worms. The other rooms are for...*other things*." The man held out his hand. "Allow me to introduce myself. My name is Mr. Tabby. I am in charge of identifying and registering each patient." He shook Pearl's hand, then shook Ben's. His sharp fingernails prickled Ben's skin. "And you are?"

"I'm Pearl Petal."

"I'm Ben Silverstein."

"Well, Pearl Petal and Ben Silverstein, before we proceed, you must sign this." The man pulled out a piece of paper from his vest pocket.

"I'm not supposed to sign anything without my mother or father reading it first," Pearl explained as she refused to take the pen Mr. Tabby offered. "I signed some papers once, and we ended up with a big satellite dish on our roof. I was grounded for two weeks. No computer. No candy. No nothing."

The man wiggled the pen. "You cannot go into the Identification Room if you do not sign this paper. If you do not sign this paper, I will have to take the hatchling and leave you here."

"I'll sign it," Ben said. He handed the cookie tin to Pearl. Then he read the paper while Pearl looked over his shoulder.

BY SIGNING THIS PAPER, I PROMISE THAT I WILL NOT BLAME DR. WOO FOR ANY INJURIES I MIGHT RECEIVE FROM AN IMAGINARY WORLD OR KNOWN WORLD CREATURE. CAUSES OF INJURY INCLUDE BUT ARE NOT LIMITED TO: BITING, SCRATCHING, CHEWING, GNAWING, VENOMOUS STINGING, HYPNOTIZING, TOSSING, IGNITING, CRUSHING, STOMPING, IMPALING, GOUGING, SHREDDING, AND VAPORIZING.

SIGNED,

X _____

"Vaporizing?" Ben asked. "Wait a minute. That sounds dangerous."

"Oh, it is dangerous. Extremely dangerous. And painful." Mr. Tabby pulled out a little device from his vest pocket and typed something on its keypad. "But according to my creature calculator, there are no vaporizing creatures currently in the hospital. The odds of your being vaporized today are zero."

"But what about these other things?" Ben asked. "Shredding? I don't want to be shredded."

"I think crushing sounds worse," Pearl said.

Mr. Tabby frowned. "I cannot guarantee your

safety. That is why you must sign the paper."
He held out the pen. "You cannot accompany the
hatchling into the Identification Room unless you
sign. Both of you."

Ben signed. Pearl hesitated but then signed.
Mr. Tabby tucked the paper into his vest pocket.
"Now, if you'll please follow—"

A roar filled the room—the kind of roar that
should be capitalized and followed by at least three
exclamation marks. *ROAR!!!* It went on for a very
long time, as if the creature making the sound had
the largest lungs in the world. Cobwebs drifted
down from the ceiling as something stomped on
the floor above.

During the roar, Ben thought about all sorts of
things. He thought he'd like to run in the opposite
direction of the roar and keep running until he
ended up back at his grandfather's house. Then
he thought that he shouldn't run, because that
would make him look like a chicken. But then he
thought that it was better to look like a chicken
than to be stomped, or crushed, or shredded.

"What was that?" Pearl asked as the roar faded.

"I dare not say." Mr. Tabby smoothed out the front of his vest. "Now, on to business." As he opened the door to the Identification Room, he said to Ben, "Would you be so kind as to bolt the front door?"

As Pearl followed Mr. Tabby into the Identification Room, the cookie tin still in her hands, Ben hurried across the lobby. He grabbed the dead bolt, but it wouldn't budge. He didn't have dead bolts in his house back in Los Angeles. Instead, there was a security keypad that activated an alarm system. Ben pinched his fingers trying to slide the rusty bolt into place. After a few tries, he gave up. The door was closed— that was good enough. Besides, he didn't want to miss one second of whatever was going on in the other room.

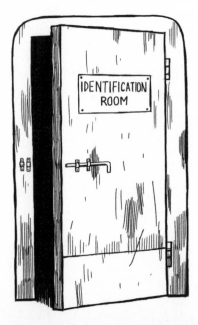

10

THE WYVERN

"Please set the patient on the identification table," Mr. Tabby said.

The table sat in the middle of a cluttered room. A wide conveyor belt ran from one end of the table to a huge hole in the wall. The hole led into a tunnel of some sort.

Mr. Tabby handed Ben and Pearl each a fire-fighter's helmet. "We must take precautions. Even a hatchling can produce a powerful flame."

"It did," Ben said. "It almost fried my face."

Mr. Tabby set a helmet on his head, then lowered

the face shield. Ben and Pearl did the same. "Step away, please." The kids stepped back as Mr. Tabby removed the lid of the cookie tin.

The baby dragon arched its neck and turned its face, looking up at Mr. Tabby. A watery hiss emerged from its mouth, but no flame. Its head fell back onto the green-stained paper towels. Mr. Tabby removed the helmet. "No need for concern. It is too weak."

Ben and Pearl took off their helmets and set them aside. Mr. Tabby slid on a pair of white gloves, then grabbed a pair of tweezers from the table drawer.

"I thought it might be a bat," Ben said.

"That is understandable. The color, the wings..." Using the tweezers, Mr. Tabby gently stretched out the bad wing. "But just as I suspected, it is a wyvern. My nose is rarely wrong."

"What's a wyvern?" Pearl asked.

"A wyvern is a winged dragon with two legs," Mr. Tabby said. "They appear in many medieval stories from the area of the Known World called

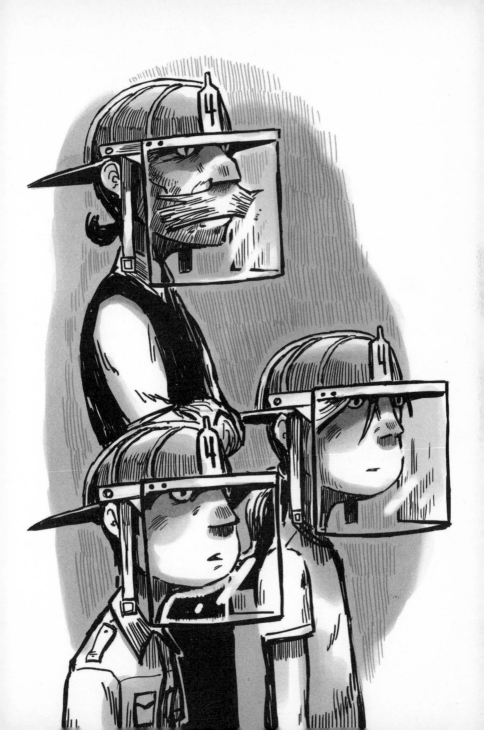

Wales. The wyvern was popular with knights in shining armor, who often wore its image on their shields and in their coats of arms." Using the tweezers, he delicately uncurled the hatchling's tail. "This sort of dragon often has a barbed tail."

"Can you fix its wing?" Ben asked.

"The wing is easily mended," Mr. Tabby said. "As is the puncture wound in the tail. Do you have any idea how it became injured?"

"My grandpa's stupid cat caught it."

Mr. Tabby narrowed his eyes at Ben. "*Stupid* cat? You dare call a cat *stupid*?" A low growl arose in Mr. Tabby's throat.

Ben thought that *stupid* was a perfectly good way to describe a cat, along with *mean*, *nasty*, and *rotten*. He didn't like cats, ever since the neighbor's cat ate his first hamster. All that had been left was the end of the hamster's tail. "I don't like cats."

Mr. Tabby's mustache flicked with annoyance. "My dear boy, perhaps cats don't like *you*."

"The baby closed its eyes again," Pearl said, pointing.

Mr. Tabby mumbled as he typed on his creature calculator. "Species: dragon. Breed: wyvern. Age: approximately three days."

"Is the other dragon its mother?" Pearl asked.

"What other dragon?"

"The one Ben and I saw flying. The one that landed on the factory roof."

"That is a bothersome question that I shall ignore," Mr. Tabby said. "This hatchling was in our nursery. The cat must have gotten in somehow."

"Probably through one of the broken windows," Pearl said.

Ben still couldn't believe they were talking about dragons. Real, living, breathing dragons. "I don't understand something," he said. "If this is a worm hospital, how come you had a baby dragon in your nursery?"

"Another bothersome question." Mr. Tabby removed the gloves. "The hatchling will need surgery to treat the broken wing and the cat bite."

"Can I have it back after the surgery?" Ben asked.

"No."

"But—"

"If I gave the hatchling to you, I would be breaking the law," Mr. Tabby said. "Creatures from the Imaginary World are not allowed to live in the Known World. Look what happened with the Loch Ness monster."

"What?" Pearl said with a gasp. "You're telling us that the Loch Ness monster is real?"

Mr. Tabby cleared his throat. "Again, I shall ignore that question."

"But the big dragon is living here," Ben pointed out. "In the...Known World."

"The *big dragon* has Dr. Woo's permission to live here. Oh dear, I shouldn't have told you that." Mr. Tabby folded his arms and stared at the two kids, who wore equal looks of surprise. "Even if I agreed to give you the hatchling, which I would not do, but even if I did, how would you take care of it?"

"I don't know," Ben said with a shrug.

"I could keep it in my bedroom," Pearl said. "I have a big bedroom."

"My dear girl, do you live in a castle?"

"No, I live above the Dollar Store."

Mr. Tabby raised a red eyebrow. "The tiny creature you see before you will grow to be fifteen feet long, with a twenty-foot wingspan and the weight of one ton. When it reaches puberty, more barbs will sprout on its tail. Flames will shoot from its snout when it is frightened, angry, or simply bored. Unless the Dollar Store is made of stone, you will have constant visits from the fire department. And then there is the issue of feeding it."

"We can make dragon's milk," Ben said. "We can use your recipe."

"The recipe will only help you for a few days. The milk must be served boiling hot, which is a dangerous feat. The hatchling will grow very quickly and will require fresh meat. Squirrels, rats, and rabbits will do at first. But a full-grown wyvern will eat a cow a day."

"Wow," Ben said. "That's a lot of meat."

"Exactly." Mr. Tabby picked up the cookie tin and set it on the conveyor belt. "I will send the wyvern to the surgery room."

"But you said that Dr. Woo is making a house call," Ben pointed out. "Who will do the surgery?"

"The splinting of a wing and the stitching of a wound are simple matters." He pressed a button, and the conveyor belt began a steady roll, carrying the cookie tin and its occupant into the tunnel. Ben wanted to grab the tin and not let it go. But he knew the baby dragon was going to get the help it needed. He and Pearl stood at the tunnel's entrance, watching until the hatchling disappeared.

"I didn't even get the chance to hold it," Pearl said sadly.

"Good-bye," Ben whispered.

"Now I will escort you two from the building. Most certainly your parents are wondering about your absence."

"I'm supposed to get home to do chores," Pearl said. "I'll be in big trouble if—"

An alarm rang and a nasal voice shot out of a

speaker that was set high in the wall. "Emergency code yellow, emergency code yellow. Sasquatch escape. All personnel needed immediately."

Pearl and Ben shared a stunned look.

Normally, someone shouting "Sasquatch escape" would have made Ben laugh. But very few "normal" things had happened since he'd come to Buttonville.

"Oh dear," Mr. Tabby said. "Well, no need to worry. As long as the front door is bolted, we should not have any cause for concern."

Ben gulped. His mind raced to the front door and its rusty bolt. "Uh..."

"Emergency code red, emergency code red," the loudspeaker voice announced. "All personnel needed immediately. Sasquatch has left the building!"

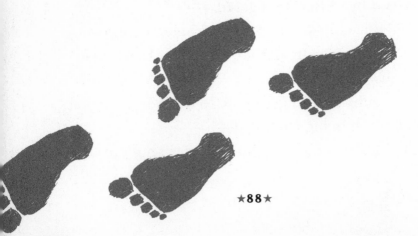

11

HAIRY ESCAPE

Mr. Tabby hurried into the lobby with Ben and Pearl at his heels. A cool breeze tickled Ben's face. The factory's front door stood wide open.

"Oops," Ben said.

"Oops?" Mr. Tabby asked, his eyes flashing.

"The bolt was rusty," Ben started to explain. "I tried, but I couldn't—"

"Do you know what you've done?" A soft growl rose in Mr. Tabby's throat. "You've made it possible for an Imaginary creature to enter the Known World."

"I didn't mean to," Ben said. He slid his hands

into his jeans pockets. "I tried to bolt it, but it jammed." He looked down at his shoes, hoping to avoid Mr. Tabby's glowing eyes. What was that on the floor? He reached down and picked up a tuft of coarse brown fur.

"A sasquatch's fingers are too thick to grip a dead bolt. That is why we put them on the doors." Mr. Tabby stood in the doorway, shaking his head slowly. "No sight of it. This is a dreadful turn of events."

"What's a sasquatch?" Pearl asked.

Ignoring the question, Mr. Tabby began to search through a pile of boxes. "It is my responsibility to keep things in order while Dr. Woo is making house calls. She will be very disappointed."

"I'm sorry," Ben said. "I tried to bolt it. Really, I did."

"What's a sasquatch?" Pearl asked again.

"It's a big, hairy ape," Ben said, holding out the tuft of fur. He remembered a TV show about a group of sasquatch hunters. But he'd thought the show was pretend.

"You mean there's a big ape running around Buttonville?" Pearl asked. "Cool."

"A sasquatch is not a big ape," Mr. Tabby said as he continued his search. "Apes are Known World creatures. Sasquatches come from the Imaginary World."

Ben stuffed the tuft into his pocket. He would be the only kid in his neighborhood who owned a genuine tuft of sasquatch fur, which was way

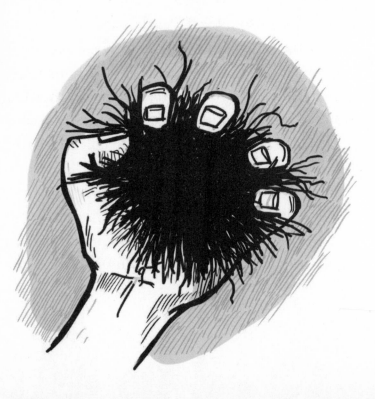

better than the shark tooth his friend Warren was always bragging about. "Don't some people call it *bigfeet*?"

"Bigfoot," Mr. Tabby corrected. "The sasquatch is also called bigfoot."

"Does it only have one foot?" Pearl asked.

Mr. Tabby moved to a different stack of boxes. "Of course it does not have only one foot. What a ridiculous question."

"Then why do they call it bigfoot instead of bigfeet?"

Mr. Tabby stopped searching and stared at Pearl. His whiskered mustache twitched with annoyance. "You are full of bothersome questions. Don't you children study Imaginary creatures in school?"

"No. Never," Pearl said. "We study real creatures. We dissected sheep eyeballs in biology."

"What a shame," Mr. Tabby said. "Your teacher would have served you better with a hydra's eyeball or a minotaur's eyeball. Sheep eyeballs are so ordinary."

"And slimy," Pearl said. "Mine slipped out of my fingers and flew across the room and landed in Ms. Bee's hair. I got detention for three days because she said I threw it on purpose. But I didn't. It slipped." She smiled mischievously at Ben.

"Ah, here it is." Mr. Tabby pulled a cardboard box from the stack and set it on the floor. Pearl and Ben gathered around as he removed the lid and lifted out a small metal box about the size of a loaf of bread. The engraved label read:

"Normally the doctor would take care of this matter, but as I mentioned earlier, she is on a house call. So, seeing as you are the one who did not bolt the door…" He thrust the kit at Ben.

Ben gulped as the box landed in his arms. "You want me to catch the sasquatch?"

"Indeed."

"For the millionth time, will someone please tell me what a sasquatch is?" Pearl demanded with a stomp of her foot.

Mr. Tabby cleared his throat. "Sasquatch, also known as bigfoot, is a large, hairy, humanoidlike creature that inhabits the forests of the Imaginary World. It has a sloping brow and a small brain. It can stand six to ten feet tall and weigh in excess of five hundred pounds." He pulled out his creature calculator. "This individual, however, stands at seven feet four inches and weighs four hundred and ten pounds. Dr. Woo is treating it for foot fungus."

"Gross," Pearl said.

Ben looked out the front door. "People will start freaking out if they see it."

"Yes, they will," Mr. Tabby said. "People always *freak out* when an Imaginary World creature steps into the Known World."

"Maybe we should call the police," Ben suggested.

"My aunt Milly is a police officer," Pearl said. "I could call her."

"That is a terrible idea," Mr. Tabby said. "Such a call would most certainly lead to tragedy. The authorities would take the sasquatch away and lock it up. And then the sasquatch would never get back to its home in the Imaginary World, where its family is waiting. You must keep this a secret. We must work together to protect the sasquatch."

Ben and Pearl nodded.

"Do not worry. The sasquatch is gentle by nature. It will not hurt anyone. Not on purpose. And it will not go far. Sasquatches are lazy. They don't like to travel. They prefer the forest and will almost always choose it as a place to hide and sleep. I suggest you begin your search there." Mr. Tabby returned the cardboard box to the pile, then smoothed out his vest. "I have much work to do while Dr. Woo is away. I will rely on you two to bring the sasquatch back to the hospital safe and sound." He held out a small brass key. "This will open the Sasquatch Catching Kit." Pearl's hand shot out faster than Ben's and grabbed the key.

And with that, Mr. Tabby turned on his polished heels and opened the EMPLOYEES ONLY door. The door closed behind him, leaving Ben and Pearl alone in the lobby.

"This has got to be the weirdest day ever," Pearl said.

"The weirdest," Ben agreed.

"Well, we'd better hurry."

12

Ben and Pearl huddled on the floor of his bedroom. Grandpa Abe was at the senior center, so Ben's bedroom provided more privacy than Pearl's bedroom, which sat above the busy Dollar Store. And when you're about to open a secret Sasquatch Catching Kit, it's best to have some privacy.

"Your hamster's cute," Pearl said as Snooze chewed on a cheese puff. "My mom won't let me have a hamster, because she says it'll make my room smell like a dirty diaper." She shrugged.

"Your room doesn't smell like a dirty diaper. Not really. Well, maybe just a little."

Ben was used to the pungent scent that drifted from the hamster cage, so he wasn't insulted. "Go on," he urged, since Pearl still had the key. "Open it."

She slid the brass key into the lock. It clicked, and the box lid sprang open. With an excited breath, Pearl pulled out the first item—a little leather-bound book: *Dr. Woo's Guide to Catching a Sasquatch*. Pearl opened the book and read the following text out loud.

This book will help you catch a sasquatch. This book will not help you catch any other two-legged creature, such as a yeti or a troll or a leprechaun. Please refer to my other guidebooks if you are trying to catch something other than a sasquatch.

"'A yeti or a troll or a leprechaun'?" Ben interrupted. "Does it really say that?" Pearl showed him the page, then continued reading.

Before trying to catch a sasquatch, there are a few things you must know.

First thing: The sasquatch is not as stupid as it looks. And it looks pretty stupid. It enjoys puzzles and likes to arrange things by color.

"Weird," Ben said.

Second thing: The sasquatch has one of the foulest odors among Imaginary creatures. Some people say it smells like a wet dog that has rolled in stinky socks.

Third thing: The sasquatch cannot speak. Therefore, it does not like to be asked questions. If you ask it too many questions, it will get angry.

Fourth thing: Although it is a gentle creature and rarely hurts a fly, do not make a sasquatch angry. It has the ability to tear off your limbs.

Fifth thing: The sasquatch loves to eat and never gets full. In the wild, it eats forest greens, berries, mushrooms, and bark. But if it escapes into the Known World, it

will seek out food that is sweet,
particularly chocolate.

Pearl looked up from the book. "I love chocolate, too. But not the kind with nuts. Everything gets ruined when you add nuts. I wonder if sasquatches like nuts."

Ben elbowed her. "Keep reading."

After much trial and error, I have found that there are three ways to successfully catch a sasquatch.

First way: Put it to sleep.

A tranquilizer dart is included in this kit. The dart contains enough potion to put an average-sized sasquatch to sleep. It is best to shoot the dart directly at the sasquatch's rump. The potion will take effect immediately.

When the sasquatch falls, anything it lands on will be crushed, so keep your distance. The potion will last for one hour. If you are unable to carry a sasquatch, do not use the tranquilizer dart.

Pearl looked up again. "How much did Mr. Tabby say our sasquatch weighs?"

"Four hundred and something pounds." Ben took out a sealed plastic tube and a blowpipe from the box. "I don't think we can carry a four-hundred-pound sasquatch." He set the tube and blowpipe aside. Pearl kept reading.

Second way: Trap it.

A net is included in this kit. I have found that if a sweet treat is placed inside the net, the sasquatch will walk right into it and will sit and eat the treat while the net is secured around it.

The sasquatch rarely puts up a fight, unless you anger it by asking a lot of questions.

If you have not arranged for transportation, and if you are unable to drag a sasquatch, then do not use the net.

"If we can't carry a four-hundred-pound sas-quatch, I don't think we'll be able to drag it," Ben pointed out. He set the net aside, then looked inside the box. Three items remained.

Third way: Feed it.

The sasquatch is always hungry and has a sweet tooth. I have found that the sasquatch will willingly follow me if I hand it pieces of chocolate. Do not run out of chocolate before you reach your destination or you will have to use one of the other methods.

"Hey, that sounds pretty easy," Ben said as he pulled out a chocolate bar. "But what's this green thing?" The item in question was the size and shape of a tennis ball.

I have also included a fog bomb, which will create a fog bank. This will provide camouflage in case you run into nosy neighbors.

Pearl reached into the box and removed the last item.

And last but not least, I have included a whistle. When used correctly, it releases a sound quite similar to the call of a wild sasquatch. Use this whistle only as a last resort and only if you are a professional, for without the proper amount of airflow, you may attract creatures other than the sasquatch.

Pearl set the book aside and held the whistle up to the light. The overhead bulb shone on the silver surface like the moon. "I wonder what the call of a wild sasquatch sounds like," she mused.

"It probably sounds like that roar we heard at the hospital," Ben said.

"You think?" Pearl rolled the whistle between her fingers, a smile tickling one side of her mouth. "I'd sure like to find out." She brought the whistle to her lips.

"Wait!" Ben cried, grabbing her wrist. "The book said to use the whistle only as a last resort."

Pearl's smile widened. "Oh, come on, Ben. Don't you want to know what a sasquatch sounds like? I'll use just a teeny-tiny bit of air. I'll blow real soft. No one will hear it but us." Then she whispered, "I'll be very quiet."

"Okay," he agreed, releasing her wrist. "As long as you're very quiet."

So Pearl put the whistle to her lips, and, with the smallest puff of air, she blew.

13

THE SCURRY

Ben leaned close, expecting a soft little growl to leak from the whistle's end.

CHIIIIIIIIIIIIRT!

He plunged his fingers into his ears. "Stop," he begged. Pearl dropped the whistle. The sound had been as loud as a train passing directly through the bedroom. Snooze squeaked and dove into his nest. The sound echoed off the walls, then faded. Ben lowered his fingers and glared at Pearl.

"I barely used any air," she insisted. Then she looked around. "Do you think anyone heard that?"

"Everyone heard that," Ben said, his ears ringing a bit. "You could hear that all the way to the airport." Then he and Pearl shared a worried look.

"Do you think…?" Pearl scrambled to her feet. "Do you think the sasquatch heard?"

"Of course it heard." Ben furrowed his brow. "But that was a weird sound. *Chirt?* I was expecting a roar."

"Me too." Pearl's shoulders stiffened as a rumbling sound arose in the distance. "What's that?"

Ben rushed to the bedroom window, threw it open, and stuck out his head. The rumbling was louder now.

"Move over," Pearl said, shoving her elbows onto the windowsill. As she stuck out her head, a lock of blond hair blew across Ben's mouth. He wiped it away. "It sounds like something very big is running this way."

Something very big? Running this way? Ben's heartbeat quickened.

A few minutes ago they were opening a metal box, excited about possibilities, and now a real, live sasquatch was running their way. Images of Godzilla filled Ben's mind. He remembered the old Japanese movies where the giant green reptile charged down the streets of Tokyo, smashing cars and buildings with its enormous feet. Only this wasn't Tokyo; this was Buttonville. And this Godzilla wasn't a giant lizard; it was a big, hairy forest-dweller!

"What do we do?" Ben asked, his voice squeaking. "We're not ready. We haven't figured out how to trap it. We haven't figured out how to get it back to the factory. We—"

"Shhhh," Pearl interrupted. "Listen."

Ben swallowed his panic and turned his ear toward the street. The rumbling grew closer, but it sounded different, more complex. "It sounds like... like a herd of cattle." He didn't remember seeing any grazing land on the drive from the airport. Just lots and lots of trees. "Do you have cattle in Buttonville?"

"No." Pearl ducked back into the bedroom and pointed at the whistle. "The book said that if the whistle wasn't used properly, it could attract other creatures."

"What kind of other creatures?" Ben whispered.

Pots and pans rattled as Ben and Pearl raced through the kitchen. Ben grabbed the knob and yanked open the front door. Then they stood side by side on the porch. The boards vibrated beneath their feet as the rumbling neared. Barnaby, who'd been sleeping in a patch of sun on the front lawn, darted up the nearest tree. Clinging to a branch, he hissed, the fur on his back standing straight up. Down the road, someone screamed. Ben clung to the porch railing as a gray mass appeared around the corner.

"Squirrels?" Pearl cried.

A scurry of squirrels charged down Pine Street. There must have been a hundred of them. Maybe more. Ben had never seen anything like this. Squirrels lived in parks back home, but they never traveled in groups, and they never raced down the street as if they were competing in a marathon. "What's happening?" Ben asked.

The scurry knocked over a garbage can, then two mailboxes, before turning into Grandpa Abe's yard. Pearl grabbed Ben's sleeve and pulled him back through the doorway. Then they slammed the door shut and stared in awe out the front window. The little critters scrambled up the porch. Some perched on the railing, some crowded on the cherry-red porch swing, and others balanced on

the windowsill, pressing their black noses against the glass. A chorus of *chirt, chirt, chirt* filled the air.

"Whoa," Ben said. "That's the same sound the whistle made."

"Only the whistle was a million times louder." Pearl gawked at the little gray faces. "They must think we have a giant squirrel in here. Maybe they think it's the squirrel queen."

It made sense. It made crazy sense.

"How do we get rid of them?" Ben asked. The window began to fog with hot little puffs of squirrel breath.

"Maybe they'll go away. We should just wait," Pearl said.

But they didn't go away. A few cars stopped. Some neighbors peeked over the fence. When the squirrel queen didn't make an appearance, the squirrels began to explore the yard. They drank from the birdbath, then overturned it. They chased Barnaby out of the tree and took over the branches, eating all the acorns and tossing the shells aside. Their little claws dug through the grass, looking for other things to eat. *Chirt, chirt, chirt.*

"That sound is really annoying," Pearl said as eighteen pairs of beady eyes stared at her through the glass. *Chirt, chirt, chirt.*

"Yeah, and they're making a huge mess." Ben didn't want his grandfather to come home and find a huge mess in his yard. "We have to do something."

It took Pearl and Ben the rest of the afternoon to get rid of the squirrels. Armed with brooms and rakes, they pushed them out of the tree and chased them down the street. Eventually, not a single gray-haired varmint remained. They set the birdbath, garbage cans, and mailboxes upright. Then Ben raked acorn shells while Pearl wiped squirrel paw prints off the window.

Just as they finished, Grandpa Abe's phone rang. Ben answered it. It was Pearl's mother, reminding Pearl to come home and finish her chores. A shipment from China had arrived, and all the merchandise needed to be put on the Dollar Store shelves.

"Can you come back later?" Ben asked. "So we can look in the forest?"

"We eat dinner after we close the store, and then it gets dark, and there's no way my mom will let me walk around the woods in the dark," Pearl said. "Guess we'll have to wait until tomorrow."

Ben agreed. The forest at night sounded a bit... scary.

Back in his bedroom, they collected the net, tranquilizer dart, blowpipe, chocolate bar, fog bomb, guidebook, and whistle and returned them to the Sasquatch Catching Kit. Before Ben could stop her, Pearl locked the kit.

"You keep the box, I'll keep the key. That way, neither one of us will do something we shouldn't." She smiled knowingly. "Like blow the whistle again."

"I wasn't going to blow the whistle," Ben said, though he had been wondering what sort of sound would emerge if he gave it a try. Would a swarm of bees appear, or maybe a sloth of bears?

"Come to the Dollar Store as soon as you can in the morning," Pearl said. "I'll wake up extra early and get all my chores done. Then we can go to the woods."

"Let's hope Mr. Tabby was right when he said the sasquatch won't hurt anyone and that it'll probably just sleep in the woods."

"Well, there's no way *I'm* going to be able to sleep tonight." She tucked the key into her pocket. "This is the most exciting thing that's ever happened to me!"

After Pearl left, Grandpa Abe returned from the senior center. "What have you been up to?" he asked.

"Just hanging out with Pearl," Ben said.

"Pearl? The troublemaker? Well, I'm glad you've made a friend." Grandpa Abe handed Ben a piece of birthday cake. "Birthday day at the senior center was fun. By the way, you've got some *schmutz* on your *punim*."

"Huh?" Ben asked.

Grandpa Abe frowned. "Isn't your father teaching you Yiddish? It means 'you've got some dirt on your face.'" He pointed to Ben's cheek. Ben wiped it with his sleeve. It was a piece of acorn shell. "And what do you have planned for tomorrow? Another day...*hanging out*?"

"Yeah." Ben smiled. He stuck his hand in his pocket and found the clump of fur. Tomorrow was sure to be a day like no other. Because the truth, for once, was better than any story he could come up with.

Tomorrow he would go looking for a sasquatch.

14

WELCOME WAGON

Ben awoke to the sounds of his grandfather shuffling around in the kitchen. Cupboards clacked, dishes clinked, a coffeepot gurgled. He threw the comforter aside, slid onto the floor, then peered beneath the bed. The Sasquatch Catching Kit sat surrounded by a crop of dust balls.

"Breakfast!" his grandfather hollered.

Ben pushed the box deeper beneath the bed. His plan was to eat breakfast as quickly as possible, then dart over to Pearl's.

"So?" Grandpa Abe asked as he poured milk

into his bowl of Sugar Loops. "Do you and Pearl want to come to the senior center? Everyone wants to meet my grandson, the storyteller. And today is pudding day. What could be better than that?"

"No, thank you," Ben said as he sat at the kitchen table.

"What? You don't like pudding? What kind of person doesn't like pudding?"

"I like pudding," Ben said. "But Pearl wanted me to meet her at the Dollar Store after breakfast." Ben poured milk into his bowl. Then he stuffed his mouth with Sugar Loops so he wouldn't have to keep answering questions.

"Well, I guess that'll be okay." Grandpa Abe tapped his spoon on the table. "Why would you want to hang out with a bunch of old people when you can hang out with a kid your own age? But just be careful. Like I told you, that girl's a troublemaker."

"Okay."

The toaster popped, and the scent of warm

bread filled the air. "You want a schmear of cream cheese on your bagel?"

As Ben nodded, a knock sounded on the front door, followed by a high-pitched voice. "Yoo-hoo!"

Grandpa Abe groaned. Then he whispered, "That voice. I know that voice. Pretend we're not home."

"Who is it?" Ben whispered back.

"Martha Mulberry, the busiest busybody in Buttonville."

Knock, knock, KNOCK. "I know you're in there, Abe Silverstein. Are you going to make me stand here all day? Because I will. I will stand here all day and knock until you open this door."

"All right, already." With another groan, Grandpa Abe grabbed his cane and hobbled across the kitchen. "Why, hello, Martha," he said in a cheerful voice after opening the front door. "How nice to see you this morning. I was just saying to my grandson, Ben, that I should have such luck as to see Martha Mulberry this morning."

Ben watched from the kitchen table as a woman

pushed her way into the living room, followed by a girl who was pulling a red wagon. They were dressed in matching red overalls and white sneakers. And they wore matching red baseball hats with the words WELCOME WAGON embroidered on the brim.

"Ben, get your *tuchus* over here and meet Mrs. Mulberry and her daughter, Victoria."

Ben shoved another spoonful of Sugar Loops into his mouth—he'd need energy for the sasquatch hunt. Then he joined his grandfather in the living room.

"Hello, Ben." Mrs. Mulberry's hair stuck out from beneath her baseball cap like frizzy ropes of red licorice. "As the president of the Welcome Wagon Committee, I'd like to officially welcome you to Buttonville." She shook Ben's hand. When she smiled, her top gums showed.

"Hi," Ben said after swallowing the Sugar Loops.

"And this is my daughter, Victoria."

The girl frowned as she shook Ben's hand. Her

eyes peered at him from behind superthick glasses. Her red hair was so frizzy it looked like it might explode from an overload of static electricity. Was this the girl Pearl had mentioned? The girl who couldn't keep a secret?

"We would have come earlier this morning, but something got into our garbage can and made a real mess," Mrs. Mulberry explained.

"Raccoons?" Grandpa Abe asked.

"No, I don't think it was raccoons," Mrs. Mulberry said. "I've never heard of raccoons sorting the garbage into colors. All the green stuff in one pile, the red stuff in another pile, and so on and so on. And it happened to six other houses on Cedar Street."

"That's very strange," Grandpa Abe said.

Ben chewed on his lower lip as he remembered the sasquatch guidebook. *It enjoys puzzles and likes to arrange things by color.*

"I was convinced that a misbehaving child did the damage," Mrs. Mulberry said. "But my neighbor Mr. Bumfrickle found a big footprint in

the grass next to his overturned garbage can."

A bigfoot print? Ben gasped and some spit went down the wrong tube.

"What's the matter with you?" Mrs. Mulberry asked as Ben started coughing. "Are you sick?"

"Nothing's the matter with me," Ben said. He hurried into the kitchen and got a glass of water. As he drank it, he imagined the sasquatch squatting in the Mulberrys' front yard, sorting through the garbage. It was supposed to be sleeping in the forest, not wandering around Buttonville. What else had the creature done during the night? He and Pearl needed to find it ASAP!

"Ben," Mrs. Mulberry called, "we have a present for you."

As Ben returned to the living room, Mrs. Mulberry grabbed a wrapped package from the wagon. "Welcome to the town of Buttonville. We hope you have a long and happy stay." She handed the package to Ben.

"Thanks," Ben said. He set the present on the sofa. "Uh, I really need to get going." But as Ben started for the door, Grandpa Abe cleared his throat.

"Ben, be a good boy and open your present."

Ben sank onto the couch, untied the red ribbon as fast as he could, and yanked open the box. It held the following things:

- *a coupon for a free movie at the Buttonville Cinema*

- *a bag of nails from the Buttonville Hardware Store*
- *a refrigerator magnet that read* **YOU GET MORE AT THE DOLLAR STORE**
- *a red baseball cap with the words* WELCOME WAGON
- *twelve ketchup packets from the Buttonville Diner*
- *a big chocolate button from the Buttonville Candy Store*

"Thanks," Ben said again.

Mrs. Mulberry stepped close to Ben. "It's my job as president of the Welcome Wagon to know everything about everybody. I understand that your parents sent you here for the summer. Why did they do that?"

Mrs. Mulberry *was* a busybody, just like Grandpa Abe had said. Ben hoped she didn't have too many questions. He turned away and looked out the window. Pearl was pacing along the sidewalk, her blond hair swishing with each step. She must have finished her chores.

"Grandpa? Can I—"

"I see Pearl Petal is waiting for you," Mrs. Mulberry said. "I noticed the two of you walking together yesterday. Are you friends?"

"I guess so," Ben said. Seeing as he and Pearl shared some pretty big secrets, it looked like they'd become friends.

"I don't like Pearl Petal," Victoria said. Her blue braces sparkled. "I never play with her."

"A wise choice." Mrs. Mulberry patted the top of her daughter's baseball cap. "That Pearl Petal is a troublemaker. You would be wise, Abe, to keep your grandson from playing with her."

"Ben's no dummy. He can choose his friends." Grandpa Abe winked encouragingly at Ben. Then he opened the front door. "So nice of you to stop by, Martha," he said with a forced smile. "I'm sure you have other things to do today."

"Yes, indeed I do." Mrs. Mulberry adjusted her baseball cap. "Someone has moved into the old button factory, and it's my job to find out who that

someone is. Even if I have to wait outside the gate all day, I must know what's going on over there."

"I'm sure you'll figure it out," Grandpa Abe said. "After all, it's your job to know everything about everybody."

Victoria grabbed the wagon's handle and followed her mother out the door. The wagon thumped down the porch steps. Victoria glared at Pearl as she passed by. Pearl glared back. Then Victoria and Mrs. Mulberry made their way along Pine Street, the wagon wheels squeaking.

"I thought they'd never leave," Grandpa Abe said. He grabbed his cane and plopped a canvas hat onto his head. "Well, you and Pearl have fun. I'm off to the senior center to help set up the tables. Pudding day is our busiest day." And off he went, tipping his hat at Pearl as he drove away.

After tucking the kit under his arm and closing the bedroom door, Ben joined Pearl outside. The cloudless sky glowed with summer sunshine. Barnaby sat on the sidewalk, pawing at a trail of ants. He'd squashed a bunch of them, and they lay

as lifeless as beads. Ben hissed a warning. "Stay away from my hamster or..." He leaned close. "Or I'll feed you to the sasquatch."

Barnaby ignored Ben. He flicked his black tail, then pounced on another ant.

"I don't think sasquatches eat cats," Pearl said. She glanced up and down the sidewalk. "I did my chores as fast as I could so I could get over here. Guess what I found out." She looked around again. "I found out that the sasquatch broke into the diner last night and ate all the ketchup packets and chocolate syrup. It left a big footprint near the door."

"And it got into a bunch of garbage cans and sorted the garbage by color," Ben told her.

Pearl took a rubber band off her wrist and pulled her hair into a ponytail. "This is serious stuff. We need to catch it before anyone sees it. Where do you think we should start looking?"

"I'm not sure." Ben shrugged. And that's when a scream filled the air. "But that sounds like a good place to start."

15

A short way down the block they found the source of the scream—an elderly lady who was leaning on the handles of her walker, her eyes staring into space as if they were made of glass.

"That's Mrs. Froot," Pearl told Ben as they ran toward her. "She's the oldest person in Buttonville. She doesn't like me because I broke her garden gnome."

"How'd you do that?" Ben asked. The contents of the Sasquatch Catching Kit jiggled with his frantic steps. He was a bit worried the motion might activate the fog bomb.

"It was an accident," Pearl explained. "I wanted to get a nest that was in Mrs. Froot's tree to add to my nest collection, but it was way up in the top branch. So I climbed the tree, but then the branch broke and I fell right on top of the gnome. Its head came off."

Mrs. Froot stood in her front yard next to her white picket fence. Dozens of colorfully painted gnomes dotted her yard as if they'd sprouted like weeds. The headless one still sat beneath the tree. Mrs. Froot's bony fingers gripped the handles of her walker as she stared down the sidewalk.

"Hello, Mrs. Froot," Pearl said. "We heard a scream."

A strangled sound emerged from Mrs. Froot's mouth, as if a word was trying to form deep down inside her. "Ssssss."

Pearl poked the lady's arm. "Are you okay?"

The sound got louder. "SSSSSS."

"I bet she's trying to say 'sasquatch,'" Ben

whispered to Pearl. "She must know where it is."

"Mrs. Froot? What did you see?" Pearl poked her again.

"Did you see something big and hairy?" Ben asked.

"Yes. Yes," Mrs. Froot said with trembling lips. "I saw a sssssss...a sssssss...a sloth."

"A sloth?" Pearl and Ben said at the same time.

Mrs. Froot finally blinked. Then she took a long, wheezy breath, and her eyes went wild, spinning around like they might fly right out of her head. "A terrible, enormous, hairy sloth right here in Buttonville. It tried to eat me."

"Are you sure it was a *sloth*?" Ben asked. He was pretty sure that sloths didn't live in North America, and he was doubly sure that if Mrs. Froot had seen something terrible, enormous, and hairy, it was most likely the escaped sasquatch. But events had been so strange lately, he couldn't be one hundred percent certain of anything.

"Tell us what happened," Pearl said.

Mrs. Froot looked up at a tree branch that

loomed overhead. "I was on my way to the senior center. It's pudding day, and I wanted to get some butterscotch before Maybell ate it all. She's always hogging the butterscotch. But I heard a strange sound, and there it was, sitting in that tree."

Ben walked around the tree, where he found a big footprint pressed into the matted grass. And there, dangling from a low branch, a tuft of brown fur. He fluffed up the grass, then grabbed the fur to hide the evidence.

"The sloth jumped out of the tree and snatched my sunbonnet right off my head. Then it ran toward Fir Street." Mrs. Froot patted her white hair. "That was my favorite sunbonnet."

Ben didn't point out to Mrs. Froot that sloths are famous for moving very slowly, not for jumping or running. If she wanted to believe that a sloth had taken her sunbonnet, then so be it. At least she didn't think it was a sasquatch.

Mrs. Froot squinted at Pearl. "Pearl Petal? Is that you? Did you do this?"

"Do what?" Pearl asked.

"Did you put a sloth in my tree?" Mrs. Froot wagged a finger at Pearl. "You have a reputation for trouble, young lady. You should stop messing around in people's trees."

"I didn't," Pearl insisted. "Really, I didn't."

"I'd better call the police," Mrs. Froot said. "They should know that there's a sloth on the loose in Buttonville!" She turned her walker and began shuffling toward her house.

"Shouldn't we stop her?" Ben asked.

"Don't worry about it," Pearl said as she started down the sidewalk. "The police will never believe her. Would you believe it if the oldest person in Buttonville told you that a sloth had jumped out of a tree and stolen her sunbonnet?"

"No," Ben said as he followed. "It kinda sounds like one of my stories."

"You write stories?" Pearl asked.

"I tell stories. I don't write them."

"Oh. You mean you lie?"

"I don't lie," Ben insisted. "I tell *stories*. There's a difference." But his mother and father had both warned him that if he kept telling his "stories" instead of telling the truth, people would stop believing anything he said.

"Look," Pearl said. She collected a tuft of brown fur that clung to a fire hydrant. They found another stuck on a rosebush. "We're on the right track."

A horn sounded, and a blue-and-white police car pulled up to the curb. The words **BUTTONVILLE POLICE FORCE** were painted on the side. "Crud. It's Aunt Milly. Act natural," Pearl told Ben.

How do you act natural when you're looking for a sasquatch? Ben wondered.

The window rolled down, and the police officer stuck out her head. "Hiya, Pearl. Who's your friend?"

"Hi, Aunt Milly." Pearl shuffled in place. "This is Ben Silverstein. He's visiting his grandpa for the summer."

"Hi," Ben said.

Officer Milly removed her dark glasses and smiled at Ben. She had the kind of smile that showed all her teeth, even the bottom ones. "Nice to meet you, Ben. Your grandpa's a swell guy. He made matzo ball soup for me when I had the flu. So, what are you two doing? You're not getting into trouble, are you?"

"No," Pearl said, hiding the sasquatch fur behind her back. "We're just...walking around."

Officer Milly eyed the metal box in Ben's hands. "You sure you're not getting into trouble?"

"I'm sure," Pearl said.

"No trouble," Ben confirmed.

"Well, okay." Officer Milly slid her glasses back on. "Hey, I got a call a few minutes ago that there's an enormous dog running around without a leash. You wouldn't know anything about that, would you, Pearl?"

"Why would I know anything about an enormous dog running around without a leash?" Pearl asked innocently. "I didn't do anything."

"Well, maybe you didn't do anything *this* time." Then Officer Milly shook her head and mumbled, "My niece, the troublemaker." And off she drove.

"How come everyone calls you a troublemaker?" Ben asked.

Pearl kicked a rock, then tucked her T-shirt into her shiny blue basketball shorts. "I don't get in trouble on purpose. I put food coloring in Mr. Mutt's koi pond because I thought it would look pretty. How was I supposed to know that it would dye the fish, too? And I set that windup rat loose during the parade because I was bored. No one ever told me that ponies are afraid of rats."

Pearl and Ben stopped at an empty intersection. Ben looked around for footprints and tufts of fur but found none. His gaze traveled up and down the street. Buttonville had to be the quietest place on Earth. No honking cars, no blaring music, no air traffic. The only sign of life was a man sweeping the sidewalk in front of the Buttonville Clothing Barn. "Hey, watch it!" the man yelled as a grocery cart rumbled past, nearly knocking him over. The rumbling grew louder as the cart rolled toward Pearl and Ben.

"That's one of our Dollar Store carts," Pearl said. "Someone's taking a ride."

"Ugh, what's that smell?" Ben asked.

The kids jumped out of the way as the cart whizzed past. A pair of hairy arms hung over the edge. A pair of hairy kneecaps and a sunbonnet peeked out the top. Thanks to the slight incline of the sidewalk, the cart picked up speed.

"The sasquatch," Ben said.

But Pearl wasn't there to hear him. She was already in pursuit.

16

The Dollar Store cart lay overturned on the steps of the Buttonville Senior Center, the sunbonnet at its side. The center's front door stood wide open. A tuft of brown fur hung from the doorknob. "Do you have the chocolate bar?" Pearl asked.

Ben, who'd been holding the Sasquatch Catching Kit the entire time, nodded. "Should we open it now?"

"Yeah. If we open it, maybe the sasquatch will smell it." Pearl unlocked the kit. Then she grabbed the chocolate bar. After tearing off the top wrapper, she folded back the foil inner wrapper. A dark, shiny rectangle peeked out. Ben wanted to take a bite.

Pearl held out the bar and quietly called, "Here, sasquatchy. Here, sasquatchy." But nothing big and hairy appeared. Only Ben's grandfather stepped out of the senior center, and he had almost no hair at all.

"Ben!" he called with a wave. "Why are you standing out there? Come in and eat some pudding."

Even though it was a nice summer morning, the senior center heat was turned on full blast. The warmth made Ben want to curl up and take a nap. He fought a yawn. This was no time to get sleepy. He and Pearl were on an important sasquatch-finding mission.

Three tables had been placed end to end, each covered with pudding cups. Some of the cups were stacked almost to the ceiling; others were displayed on cake stands. Vanilla, banana, chocolate, butter-scotch, and swirl were squeezed onto every square inch of the tables. Between the cups stood cans of whipped cream and tubs of sprinkles.

"Wow," Ben said to his grandfather. "That's a lot of pudding."

"That's a lot of pudding?" Grandpa Abe chuckled. "You should see how much pudding we had before Maybell got here." He nodded toward a rather beefy woman who was seated at the back of the room. She peeled the top off her butterscotch pudding. Dozens of empty cups littered the floor around her.

Tables and chairs crowded the rest of the room. In each chair sat a very old person. Many had hearing aids in their ears; most wore thick eyeglasses. Each had a pudding cup or two. Some of the seniors looked older than Ben's grandfather by dozens of years, their faces wrinkled like pieces of fabric.

"Do you see it?" Pearl whispered in Ben's ear.

"No," Ben whispered back. "But I can smell it." The sour odor of wet dog hung in the air, mixed with the sweet scents of banana and vanilla. Where was the hairy beast?

★143★

Because the room was buzzing with conversation, Grandpa Abe had to clap his hands to get attention. "Look, everyone!" he called. "It's my grandson, Ben."

Plastic spoons were lowered and heads turned, causing a ripple in the sea of white and silver hair. A chorus of "Hello, Ben" filled the room, along with a chorus of "What did he say?"

"And you all know Pearl," Grandpa Abe said.

A chorus of "Hello, Pearl" filled the room, along with a chorus of "What did he say?"

"Most everyone here used to work at the old button factory," Grandpa Abe told Ben. Then he pointed to the metal box in Ben's arms. "Whatcha got there?" He read the label. "Sasquatch Catching Kit. What are you two up to?"

"Uh..." Ben thought about making up a story, but even if he'd had an hour or two to come up with something fantastic, it wouldn't have been better than the truth. "We're hunting sasquatch," he said.

"And why is Pearl holding that chocolate bar in the air?"

"Because sasquatches like chocolate," Ben said.

"We're supposed to keep it a secret," Pearl hissed in Ben's ear. "Why did you tell him?"

"Don't worry. He'll think it's just one of my stories," Ben whispered.

And sure enough, Grandpa Abe rubbed his shiny head and chuckled. "I should live so long to see a sasquatch. My grandson, the storyteller." Then he gave Ben a gentle shove toward the pudding tables. "Go on. Eat."

Once again, the room filled with conversation as the seniors began to discuss matters of importance, such as hip surgery, pigeon-feeding, and napping. Pearl grabbed a banana pudding cup, ripped off the top, and started eating. "I love these things," she said as she looked around. Then she nudged Ben. "You look on that side of the room, and I'll look on this side of the room."

Ben took a cup of vanilla pudding, but he didn't eat it. Instead, he sniffed the air. The wet dog scent grew stronger as he walked to the back of the room.

"Hey," an old man said. "There's a clump of hair in my pudding." Ben hurried to the man's side. Sure enough, it was a big brown clump.

Another old man, who was seated next to Maybell, opened a cup of chocolate pudding and held it under the table. "This doggy sure likes pudding," the man said.

"I don't know why you're wasting perfectly good pudding on a dog," Maybell said as she opened a new cup. "Dogs should eat dog food, not people food. And pudding is people food."

"But it's a nice doggy," the man said.

Doggy?

Squatting, Ben lifted the hem of the tablecloth and peered under the table. The stench nearly knocked him over, as if he'd been smacked by a sweat-drenched sock. There, right next to a pile of empty pudding cups, was a pair of enormous, hairy feet.

17

FOG DAY

Ben's gaze traveled up a pair of hairy legs and up a hairy torso, and came to a rest on a pair of brown eyes. The eyes themselves were not hairy, but they were surrounded by hair. The sasquatch was wedged tight beneath the table. It looked at Ben. It blinked. Ben's heart nearly stopped beating. He was face-to-face with a living, breathing bigfoot—a creature that was supposed to exist only in stories!

It looked half ape, half caveman. Its brown fur was thick and matted with sticks and leaves. Its feet were so big they could easily fit into clown shoes. Looking at its low, sloping forehead and unibrow, Ben could see why others might think it wasn't very smart. He stiffened, expecting it to growl or show its teeth, but instead it held out a smooth brown palm and grunted. It wanted something.

"What do...?" Then Ben remembered the warning from Dr. Woo's guidebook about not asking a sasquatch questions. His heart pounding like a kettledrum, he cautiously reached out and handed the sasquatch his vanilla pudding cup.

It snatched the cup and, with two quick sweeps of its tongue, licked it clean. Just like Dr. Woo had written in her guidebook, the creature seemed to love sweet things.

"I can't find it anywhere. How can a four-hundred-pound sasquatch disappear?" Pearl asked as she knelt next to Ben. "Whatcha looking at? Oh, *wow!*" Pushing aside some empty butterscotch pudding cups, Pearl squeezed between the old man's chair and Maybell's chair to get a better look. Then she reached out and touched the sasquatch's leg.

It didn't seem to mind. Ben couldn't believe she'd
touched it. Was that courage or curiosity?

"They think it's a dog," Ben told her as the old
man tossed another cup under the table. "They
can't see very well."

"A dog?" Pearl smiled. "That's so funny." She
laughed. "That's one of the funniest things I've
ever heard."

"Well, it won't be funny if they find out it's not a dog. How are we going to get it out of here?"

The sasquatch burped. Then it sniffed the air. Its brown eyes rested on the chocolate bar in Pearl's hand. Pearl shook the bar. "You want—?"

"*Don't* ask it questions," Ben reminded her. Making the sasquatch angry would just complicate matters. He imagined it stomping through the senior center, old people screaming and fleeing in its wake. "Give it a piece."

Pearl broke off a corner of the chocolate bar and tossed it. The sasquatch caught the chocolate chunk, shoved it into its mouth, and grunted again. Then it shifted onto its knees and began to crawl toward Pearl and Ben. "Dr. Woo was right," Pearl said as she backed away. "We can tempt it with chocolate." She shook the bar again. "Here, sasquatchy, sasquatchy."

The creature crawled out from under the table. As it squeezed its enormous body between the two chairs, Maybell's fell over backward. Her sensible shoes stuck up in the air. Ben scrambled to his feet and tried to upright Maybell, but she was too heavy for him to lift.

Pearl moved quickly, waving the chocolate bar as she led the way between tables of seniors who were busy chatting and eating pudding. As the sasquatch crawled after Pearl, it knocked the seniors over like bowling pins. Chairs toppled. Pudding cups and spoons flew, as did eyeglasses, hairpieces, and a pair of dentures. "Whoa!" "Help!" "Whoopsy daisy!"

"Ben?" his grandfather called from across the room. "What's going on over there? Is that a dog? *Oy vey!* Who let a dog in here?"

"Sorry," Ben told Maybell, though she didn't seem to mind being upside down. She'd found another pudding cup and was enjoying its creamy goodness. Ben wove around the flailing arms and legs, trying to catch up to Pearl and the sasquatch. Pearl had almost reached the back door. They were so close to making their escape. But Grandpa Abe had grabbed his cane and was heading straight for

Pearl. Ben's heart thumped wildly. He needed to create some sort of distraction.

He opened the Sasquatch Catching Kit and pulled out the fog bomb. How did it work? There were no instructions attached, and even if there had been, there was no time to read them. It made fog, right? That's why it was called a fog bomb. He took hold of the little cord that hung from the green ball. But was it safe to activate it inside a building? Maybe not. Or maybe so. Sweat dotted the back of Ben's neck. The sasquatch stopped to lick something off the floor. Pearl jumped up and down, madly waving the chocolate bar. Grandpa Abe was getting closer and closer....

Ben didn't mean to pull the cord. His brain was still arguing with itself about whether it was safe to activate a fog bomb inside a room, especially a room filled with very old people. But he was scared, and sometimes, when riddled with fear, the body doesn't wait for the brain to finish its debate. And so his fingers pulled the cord.

"Uh-oh," he whispered as a plume of fog instantly shot out of the green ball, rising straight to the ceiling. Then it spread wide, filling the senior center with an instant fog bank. Cool mist settled on Ben's face. The scent of the sea drifted up his nostrils. The only thing missing was the sound of a foghorn in the distance. Grandpa Abe and the room itself disappeared. But so did Pearl and the sasquatch.

Everyone started talking at once. "Henrietta? Where have you gone?" "Why can't I see anything?" "Is this a dream?" "It's not a dream. It's fog." "Henrietta, I can't find you." "This is pudding day, not fog day." "Where am I?" "Henrietta, I love you!"

"Ben!" Pearl called from the floor. "It's clear down here."

Ben dropped to his knees. He had a perfect view down there because the fog bank floated about two feet off the ground. By pushing the kit along the floor, he managed to crawl to the exit. Pearl and the sasquatch were already outside by the time he got there.

"Phew!" Ben said as the door closed behind him. "We almost got caught."

Ben thought Pearl might say something like, "Wow, that was really smart to use that fog bomb," but she didn't say anything. She stood, her neck craned, staring at the sky. The sasquatch towered next to her, its face also turned upward.

Ben slowly rose to his feet. This time he didn't wonder what sort of bird it was. This time he didn't feel silly for thinking it was a dragon. It circled lazily, then dove behind some trees.

"It's going to the factory," Pearl said.

This was the first time Ben had seen the sasquatch standing at its full height. "How are we going to get it back to the factory without people seeing it?" he asked. "We don't have another fog bomb."

"I'm not sure," Pearl said. "It's huge!"

Ben didn't know why, but he didn't feel afraid of the gigantic beast. Maybe because it wasn't growling at him. Or maybe because it wasn't glaring at him. Or maybe because it was scratching one of its feet

and whimpering. Then it scratched the other foot. It whimpered, then scratched some more. "Mr. Tabby said Dr. Woo was treating it for foot fungus," Ben remembered. "It probably needs its medicine."

That's when a siren's howl filled the air. The sasquatch's hands flew to its ears as the howl grew louder. Ben peered around the side of the senior center. Fog leaked out the front door as a Buttonville Police Force car pulled up to the curb. A woman with dark glasses stepped out. "It's your aunt Milly," Ben said.

"We need to get out of here." Pearl looked up at the sasquatch. "We're going to take you home," she told it. "Do you—?"

"Don't ask it questions," Ben reminded her.

"Right." She broke off another chocolate chunk. "We can avoid the streets and sidewalks by cutting through the forest." She handed the chunk to the sasquatch. It popped the chunk into its mouth. "Let's go."

18

BAD BERRIES

"Sometimes I ride my bike back here," Pearl explained as she led the way down an overgrown trail. "This path will take us straight to the factory."

To Ben, a boy who had spent most of his life in the city and on the beach, the forest felt like an eerie place. The sun trickled through the leaves, casting weird shadows. Strange sounds rustled among the treetops. Dr. Woo's guidebook had said that sasquatches live in the forest, and Ben could see why. If the sasquatch stood still, it would probably look like a tree trunk and blend right in. But because it was following a girl who was feeding it chunks of chocolate, it didn't blend in at all.

"Go easy on the chocolate," Ben told Pearl. "We can't run out before we get there."

"I know, I know," Pearl said as she handed the sasquatch another piece. The creature seemed perfectly happy stomping along, collecting the offerings. Ben was starting to get used to its nasty scent, the same way he'd gotten used to the scent of hamster droppings.

"You know what I don't understand?" Ben said. "If this thing lives in the Imaginary World, then how did it get here? And where, exactly, is the Imaginary World?"

"When we meet Dr. Woo, let's ask her," Pearl said.

"You think we'll get to meet her?"

"Sure. We've rescued the sasquatch. The least she can do is thank us. Maybe she'll give us a cool reward."

Pearl stopped walking. The sasquatch stopped

walking. Ben, who was trying to imagine what kind of reward might come from the mysterious Dr. Woo, bumped right into the sasquatch's leg. "What—?"

"Shhhhh," Pearl hissed, a finger to her lips.

The sasquatch put a finger to its lips and repeated, "Shhhhh."

They'd reached the edge of the forest. The wrought-iron fence was across the street, and just beyond the fence stood the old factory.

"Oh no," Ben said when he spotted the red wagon and the two people in their red overalls and red baseball caps. "It's that lady and her daughter."

"Mrs. Mulberry and Victoria Mulberry," Pearl said through clenched teeth.

The Mulberrys peered between the bars of the locked gate. A wrapped present waited in the back of the welcome wagon, its glossy red bow sparkling in the sunshine. While Victoria yawned, Mrs. Mulberry glanced at her watch and paced. "Someone is sure to come in or out," she told her daughter. "I want to meet this Doctor...Doctor..."

"Woo," Victoria said, pointing to the sign that hung from the gate.

"I want to meet this Dr. Woo before anyone else meets this Dr. Woo," Mrs. Mulberry said. "As president of the Welcome Wagon, it's my job to know everything before anyone else knows anything."

"She's a worm doctor," Victoria said, pointing to the sign again.

"I *know* she's a worm doctor," Mrs. Mulberry snapped. "I can read that she's a *worm doctor*. What I want to know is, where did she come from? How long will she be staying? And, most importantly, what are her secrets? I must know her *deepest* secrets."

"You are the best at finding out secrets," Victoria said. "No one else in Buttonville can find out secrets the way you can."

"It's true, it's true," Mrs. Mulberry said. She stuck her thumbs under her overall straps and pushed out her chest. "I can smell a secret a mile away."

"Drat," Pearl said as she peered over a huckleberry bush. "If Mrs. Mulberry sees the sasquatch,

then she'll tell the whole town. She's the biggest gossip on the planet. How are we going to get past her?"

"I'm not sure," Ben said from behind the same bush. "There's no way we can sneak around them. I wish we had another fog bomb."

Just as he said that, the sasquatch swatted at a fly, breaking a branch in the process. Victoria Mulberry spun around and looked through her superthick lenses toward the forest.

"Uh-oh," Ben said. "I think she saw us." Both he and Pearl grabbed the sasquatch's arm and pulled it behind a tree. As they did so, the sasquatch snatched the last piece of chocolate from Pearl's hand and ate it, wrapper and all.

"Mom, did you hear that?"

"Do not bother me, Victoria. I'm watching the front door." Mrs. Mulberry squinted through a pair of binoculars.

"But something's up there in the forest," Victoria said.

"What?"

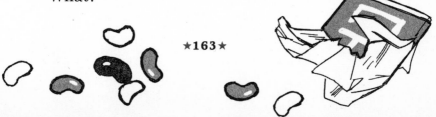

"I don't know. But it looked big and hairy."

"Is it Dr. Woo?" Mrs. Mulberry dropped her binoculars and called, "Yoo-hoo! Dr. Woo? Is that you?"

"And I think I saw Pearl Petal," Victoria said.

"Pearl Petal?" Mrs. Mulberry yanked her baseball cap off her head. Her frizzy hair shot toward the sky. "We can't let that troublemaking Pearl Petal learn Dr. Woo's secrets before we learn Dr. Woo's secrets!"

Pearl peered around the tree. "Here they come. What else do we have in that kit? What about the tranquilizer dart?"

"We can't use that on a person," Ben said. They couldn't, could they? "Besides, we only have one dart, and there are two of them. All that's left is the net."

Pearl smiled wickedly. "Net?"

Ben set the Sasquatch Catching Kit on the forest floor and opened it. After pulling out the net, he read its instruction label.

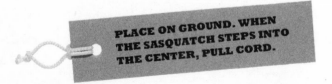

PLACE ON GROUND. WHEN THE SASQUATCH STEPS INTO THE CENTER, PULL CORD.

It sounded easy. But Mrs. Mulberry and Victoria Mulberry were people, not sasquatches. "Uh, Pearl, I'm not so sure we should do this. What if Mrs. Mulberry gets mad?"

"Of course she'll get mad," Pearl said. "But that isn't important. We have a sasquatch to save, remember?"

They both looked up at the sasquatch. It had found Dr. Woo's guidebook in the kit and was thumbing through the pages. It grunted and pointed to a drawing.

"Yeah, that looks like you," Pearl told it. The sasquatch grunted again. Chocolate specks glistened on its yellow teeth as it smiled. Pearl whispered to Ben, "It's kinda like a big teddy bear."

"Uh, it's *nothing* like a big teddy bear," Ben said, thinking that the last thing he'd want decorating his bed was a creature with greasy, moss-covered fur and itchy foot fungus.

Pearl reached up and freed a trapped beetle from the sasquatch's chest fur. Then she cooed in a baby voice. "You're a nice sasquatch. Yes you are.

You're a very nice sasquatch. We won't let those mean Mulberrys get you. No we won't." Ben rolled his eyes.

"Yoo-hoo!"

Ben clutched the net and took a long, deep breath. When his parents found out that he'd trapped the president of the Buttonville Welcome Wagon and her daughter in a net, they'd explode. But saving a sasquatch seemed a million times more important than anything else at that moment. So Ben reached around the tree and threw the net onto the ground. Holding tight to the cord, he held his breath as Mrs. Mulberry and Victoria hurried down the path.

19

HAIRY RETURN

"It smells bad in here," Victoria said. She pinched her nose as she hurried up the path.

"Do you see Dr. Woo?" Mrs. Mulberry cupped her hands around her mouth. "*Yoo-hoo!* We have a welcome present for you, Dr. Woo!"

If either of the Mulberrys had been looking down at the path, they would have clearly seen the net. There'd been no time for Ben to camouflage it by throwing leaves or dirt over it. But since Mrs. Mulberry and her daughter were looking around for Dr. Woo, they walked right into the trap. Ben yanked the cord.

"Mom?" Victoria asked as the sides of the net rose up around her. "What's happening?"

"I don't know," Mrs. Mulberry said. "Is the ground moving?"

After another yank, the net closed over their heads.

"Mom, we're trapped!" Victoria's hat fell off as she kicked at the netting. Then her feet became tangled.

"Help!" Mrs. Mulberry cried. As she struggled, her feet also became tangled. She and Victoria toppled over.

"Where are my glasses?" Victoria cried. "I can't see anything."

"Your hair is in my face. I can't see anything, either."

"Now," Ben whispered. As Victoria and her mother struggled to get back on their feet, Ben and Pearl grabbed the sasquatch's arm and tried to pull it out of the forest. But it wouldn't budge.

"I don't have any more chocolate," Pearl realized. "We need something sweet."

"Victoria, your elbow is in my ear!"

"I'm sorry, Mom. But I can't see your ear if I don't have my glasses."

"Get off me, Victoria. I can't breathe."

"I can't get off you, Mom. I'm all tangled in this stupid net."

There was no time to lose. Ben ran across the street and ripped open the Welcome Wagon present, hoping it would be just like the one he'd received earlier that morning. He shuffled through the contents—the movie coupon, the bag of nails—until he found what he was looking for. He grabbed the big chocolate button, tore off its foil wrapper, then held it up in the air. "Here, sasquatchy. Here, sasquatchy."

With a happy grunt, the sasquatch emerged from the forest. Holding out its hands, it lumbered toward Ben. Pearl gathered the Sasquatch Catching Kit and followed. "They didn't see a thing," she announced as Ben broke off a piece of the chocolate button and tossed it. "That was so much fun! Let's trap someone else!"

Ben was about to tell Pearl that he didn't think trapping someone else was a good idea when a voice said, "Excellent work."

At first, Ben thought the sasquatch had chosen this moment to begin a conversation. But a jingling sound directed Ben's attention to the other side of the gate, where Mr. Tabby was fiddling with a ring of keys. "I see Dr. Woo's Sasquatch Catching Kit came in handy," Mr. Tabby said as he unlocked and opened the gate.

Ben waved the chocolate button in the air. The sasquatch grabbed the Welcome Wagon present and followed Ben through the gate. As soon as Pearl was also inside, Mr. Tabby locked the gate.

"Help! Help!" Mrs. Mulberry cried from the forest.

"Someone needs to untangle them," Ben said.

"I shall make an anonymous phone call to the local police and let them know that assistance is required," Mr. Tabby said as he led them up the driveway. "In the meantime, we must get inside quickly, before someone else comes along."

The chocolate button lasted right up until they stepped safely into the old factory. Mr. Tabby slid the rusty dead bolt into place. "Dear, dear, what a worrisome morning." He took the metal box, with its tranquilizer dart, blowpipe, guidebook, and whistle, and set it aside. The sasquatch bent over and scratched its feet.

"You've been a very bad sasquatch," Mr. Tabby told it. "Now go on, get back upstairs. You need more medicine."

Mr. Tabby pushed the elevator button. The doors swooshed open, and the sasquatch stepped inside. With what remained of the Welcome Wagon present tucked under its arm, it turned and waved to the kids. They waved back. As the doors closed, Ben wondered what the sasquatch would do with the bag of nails, the movie coupon, the refrigerator magnet, and the other things.

Mr. Tabby pulled out his creature calculator. "Sasquatch caught," he said as he typed.

A loudspeaker, set high in the wall, crackled, and a nasal voice said, "Emergency code deactivated. Emergency code deactivated. Sasquatch has returned to the building."

Ben and Pearl took long, relieved breaths and smiled at each other. They'd done it!

"You may go now," Mr. Tabby said with a dismissive wave of his hand.

Go? Was it over? Ben's shoulders slumped.

"Wait a minute," Pearl said. "We just brought back a sasquatch. And we did it without anyone in town seeing it. Don't we get a reward or something?"

"Reward?" A low growl vibrated in Mr. Tabby's throat.

Ben's face started to feel hot. "Uh, we don't need a reward. I'm the reason the sasquatch escaped. It was my fault."

"Well, it wasn't my fault," Pearl said. She put her hands on her hips and stared right into Mr. Tabby's half-moon eyes. "I know this isn't a worm hospital. I'm not stupid. I know you have a dragon living on your roof. And I know about the hatchling and the sasquatch. I want to meet Dr. Woo, and I want to ask her some questions. That can be my reward." She nudged Ben with her elbow. "*Our* reward."

"That's not possible," Mr. Tabby said. "Dr. Woo does not speak to anyone. She's—"

The loudspeaker crackled, and a soft voice said, "Send them to my office."

20

DR. WOO

The elevator still smelled like sasquatch, even though the creature was long gone. Ben tapped his feet nervously as he and Pearl rose to the second floor. "Take a left," Mr. Tabby had told them. "Dr. Woo's office is the last room at the very end of the hall. Do not open any doors along the way. This you must promise."

"We promise," both Ben and Pearl had vowed.

There were no windows in the second-floor hallway, and no overhead lights. The only light trickled from the end of the hall, where a door stood open. "That must be her office," Ben whispered.

Pearl led the way, her steps confident and loud, her ponytail swinging. They passed door after door, all closed. Ben wondered if the sasquatch was behind one. Or the dragon hatchling. Or another equally amazing creature. But he'd promised not to open any doors, so he kept his hands tucked into his jeans pockets.

About halfway down the hall, Pearl's footsteps slowed. Then she stopped walking. "My mom and dad will be wondering where I am," she whispered. "Maybe we should leave."

Even in the dim light, Ben could see that Pearl's eyes were as wide as golf balls. "You're the one who wanted to meet her," he said, his voice hushed.

"I know. But I'm kinda scared. What if she's mean?"

He wasn't going to admit that he also felt a bit scared. He figured that a doctor who worked with dragons had to be fierce, strong—maybe even a bit crazy. "Don't you want to find out about the Imaginary World?"

Pearl nodded. But she didn't budge.

"Come on," Ben said. "We'll walk together." And so, with matching footsteps, they started walking again. A few moments later, they arrived at the open doorway.

"Come in," a gentle voice said.

Sunlight streamed in through Dr. Woo's windows, which overlooked a small lake. The water sparkled, the factory reflecting on its calm surface. The office itself was a mess, cluttered with baskets, crates, and moving boxes. A huge wooden desk, its legs carved like dragons, sat in the center of the room. Papers and books covered the desktop. Glass jars filled with cloudy liquids and odd floating things crowded the shelves.

A woman stood next to a coatrack, unbuttoning a white laboratory coat. As she hung the coat on a hook, yellow glitter drifted through the air. The woman shook her head, and glitter fell from her long black hair. She removed her stethoscope and set it on the desk. Then she folded her hands behind her back and gazed at the kids. "You wanted to see me?"

Ben held his breath. Dr. Woo was nothing like he'd imagined. She wasn't a towering superhero. She stood about his height, which wasn't very tall. Her face was as pale as the moon, her almond-shaped eyes as black as ink. She was beautiful, even with the big scar that ran across one cheek. Another ran down her neck.

"Hi," Pearl said. Then she nudged Ben. He released his breath.

"Hi," he said.

"Please, sit down."

Ben settled on a stack of boxes, as did Pearl.

After brushing yellow glitter from her skirt, Dr. Woo sat at her desk and faced the kids. "I've just returned from a house call, so I haven't had time to clean up the fairy dust."

"Fairy dust?" Pearl whispered.

Dr. Woo tapped her fingers on her desk. Her right index finger was missing. Ben remembered the paper he and Pearl had signed about not blaming Dr. Woo if something crushed, stomped, vaporized, or bit them. Had something bitten off Dr. Woo's finger?

"Mr. Tabby informed me that you were sent to retrieve the sasquatch," Dr. Woo said. "Clearly you've been successful."

"Yes," Ben said. "I'm sorry I didn't bolt the door. It was my fault it got out."

"I also understand that you found our missing wyvern hatchling."

"Yes," Ben said again. "My grandpa's cat hurt it. I'm sorry about that, too."

"Did you say *fairy* dust?" Pearl asked. "Fairies are *real*?"

Dr. Woo didn't answer that question. Instead, she stifled a yawn. "Excuse me. I've had a long journey, and I need to get some sleep." She leaned back in her chair. "What is it you wished to see me about?"

Pearl looked at Ben. He nodded encouragingly. She scooted to the edge of the box and spat out the following questions at rocket speed. "Who are you? And where is the Imaginary World? And how do you get to it? And how come no one else knows about it? And if dragons really exist, then how come everyone says they don't? And if there are sasquatches and dragons, then are fairies real? And what about unicorns? 'Cause I'd really like to meet a unicorn. Can I meet a unicorn? And why do you have yellow glitter in your hair? And"—she paused for a millisecond—"can we go to the Imaginary World with you?" She took a long breath, then closed her mouth.

Silence filled the room. Ben could barely keep himself from wiggling as they waited for the doctor's answers.

Dr. Woo suddenly sat up very straight. "It is always a challenge to keep my hospital a secret, and you two already know more than you should." Her gentle voice turned dark and serious. Something flashed in her eyes. "I'm not sure what to do about it."

Were they in trouble? Ben shifted nervously. Was Dr. Woo going to tell his parents that he'd caused that big mess in the senior center? And that he'd captured the Mulberrys with a net? "You don't have to do anything," he said. "We won't tell anyone about the hospital."

"That's right," Pearl said. "And we won't tell anyone about the sasquatch."

"Or the hatchling," Ben said.

"We promise," Pearl said.

"Yeah, we promise."

Dr. Woo did not appear convinced by these eager promises, for her brow remained furrowed, her lips pursed. She looked from Ben to Pearl and back to Ben. Ben smiled, trying to look like a boy who always told the truth—not like a boy who made up stories. What was the doctor thinking? She looked at Pearl again. Pearl smiled, too, the big gap looking like a piece of black licorice stuck between her teeth.

Dr. Woo pressed a button on her desk intercom. "Mr. Tabby? We have a serious breach in security. Do you have any suggestions?"

Mr. Tabby's voice drifted from the speaker. "We could have the dragon carry them away and leave them somewhere, a mountaintop perhaps, or a deserted island."

"That is an option," Dr. Woo said. "But what if they were rescued? They'd still know our secrets."

"Very true. Hmmmmm." Mr. Tabby paused for a moment. Ben was about to assure Dr. Woo, once again, that he'd tell no one about the hospital when Mr. Tabby said, "I have a brilliant idea. We could leave them with the cyclops. He's always hungry."

"You've got a cyclops?" Pearl asked. "That's so amazing."

Ben couldn't believe Pearl was more interested in the fact that Dr. Woo *had* a cyclops than the

fact that she might *feed* the kids to the cyclops. "Uh"—he slid off the boxes, then took a couple of steps backward—"I think we'd better be going."

"I don't think feeding them to the cyclops is a good idea," Dr. Woo told Mr. Tabby. "Too messy."

"Too messy?" Ben mumbled. How far was that elevator? If he made a run for it, could he get there before Dr. Woo changed her mind?

"And if the children went missing, we'd have to deal with the local police. There must be a better way to handle this situation," Dr. Woo said.

"Hey," Pearl said as she also slid off the boxes. "What are you talking about? You don't need to do anything. Ben and I promised. We *promised*."

Once again, Dr. Woo's gaze traveled from Ben to Pearl and back to Ben. "I wonder..." She leaned her elbows on the table. "I wonder..." She tapped her fingers again. "I've only done this one other time, but I wonder if..."

Ben took a few more steps backward. He was in the doorway now, his legs poised and ready to bolt if the dreaded words *feed them to the* came out of Dr. Woo's mouth.

"Mr. Tabby?" Dr. Woo said.

"Yes?"

"I think I have the solution." Dr. Woo's face relaxed. "They seem like nice kids. And it takes skill and cunning to catch a sasquatch. Since they already know too much, and since we could use some extra hands around here..." She smiled. "I will make them my apprentices."

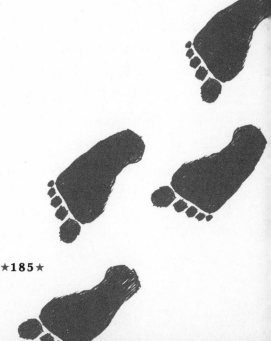

21

SECRET KEEPERS

What?" Pearl said with a gasp. "You want us to be your apprentices? Really? That's so cool!"

Ben stepped back into the room. "Apprentices?"

"That's right," Dr. Woo said.

"I'll do it!" Pearl cried. "When can I start? Can I start right now?"

Mr. Tabby, who remained on the other end of the intercom, cleared his throat. "Dear me, dear me. Are you certain you want the responsibility of two children? Human children require so much care. They do not respond well to commands. Their curiosity leads them astray time and time again."

"They won't be my responsibility," Dr. Woo said. "Since you are my assistant, they will be your responsibility."

"Oh." Mr. Tabby's voice turned cold. "More work for me. How *delightful*." Then the intercom went silent.

Pearl nudged Ben with her elbow. "Can you believe this? Apprentices!"

Ben's legs wobbled with excitement. Apprentice to a veterinarian for Imaginary creatures? He could hardly believe it. But then he remembered. "I don't think I can do it," he said, disappointment settling over him like a rain cloud. "I'm only here for the summer. Then I go back to Los Angeles."

"I'm not going to Los Angeles," Pearl said. "I live here. I never go anywhere. I can do it for sure."

"You can both do it," Dr. Woo said. "We can make this a summer apprenticeship, to begin with. But you must get permission from your parents."

"What do we tell them?" Ben asked.

"Tell them that you will be working at Dr. Woo's Worm Hospital. I will expect you to be here Monday, Wednesday, and Friday. I will expect you to arrive each morning at eight AM precisely, and you will leave at three PM precisely." She shuffled through a desk drawer, then slid a piece of paper to the edge of the desk, along with a pen. "But first you must sign the contract of secrecy."

Another thing to sign? Pearl didn't argue this time. She signed immediately. Ben leaned over the paper, squinting. "The print is really small. I can't read any of it."

Dr. Woo pushed the pen toward Ben. "It simply states that you will not tell anyone that this is actually a hospital for Imaginary creatures. And that anything you see, hear, feel, touch, smell, or taste while working as my apprentice will be kept a secret."

Ben thought about it. As cool as the apprenticeship sounded, eight o'clock in the morning was really early. He'd never been a morning person. He had two alarms in his bedroom back home just so he wouldn't be late for school. Monday, Wednesday, *and* Friday were a lot of days. And then there was the whole crushing, shredding, vaporizing thing. "What will we be doing?" he asked, staring at Dr. Woo's missing finger.

"You'll be doing whatever needs to be done," Dr. Woo replied. A few stray pieces of yellow glitter fell from her hair.

"Come on," Pearl said. "Sign it. What are you waiting for? What else are you going to do all summer? Hang out at the senior center?"

Ben picked up the pen. Had he already broken the contract of secrecy by telling Grandpa Abe he was searching for sasquatches? But his grandfather hadn't believed him, so no harm had been done. He signed, Ben Silverstein.

Dr. Woo collected the contract and tucked it in

the top desk drawer. Then her expression and voice turned serious again. "There are consequences for breaking the contract," she told them. "Just so you know."

Before Ben could ask what kind of consequences, a buzzer sounded and the same nasal voice shot out of the loudspeaker. "Dr. Woo, the hatchling is scheduled for departure."

"Thank you. I'll be right there." Dr. Woo stood. She collected her lab coat from the rack and slid her arms through its white sleeves. Sunlight streamed in through the window, illuminating the scar on her face and casting a shadow that made it look twice as large.

"Are you sending the hatchling back to the Imaginary World?" Pearl asked. "Can we see it before it leaves?"

"Can we say good-bye?" Ben asked.

Dr. Woo gathered her long hair and tied it into a knot at the back of her neck. Then she slid her stethoscope over her head. "Dragon hatchlings become easily attached to humans. It is best that it not see you."

Too bad, Ben thought. He wished he'd taken a picture of the hatchling when he'd found it, before he'd signed that contract of secrecy. Now he'd never see the little sea horse face again.

"Sometimes the hardest part of this job is saying good-bye," Dr. Woo said, as if reading Ben's mind. Then she ushered them to the elevator door. "Mr. Tabby will see you to the gate. Good day."

Mr. Tabby was waiting in the lobby, a pocket watch in his hand. "So? You are going to be apprentices?"

"Maybe," Ben said. "If we can get permission."

Mr. Tabby tucked the watch into his vest pocket. "Today is Saturday. The apprenticeship begins on Monday. That gives you one day to get permission."

"We'll get it," Pearl said with a confident nod.

"Follow me. It's time for you to go home." The big ring of keys swung from Mr. Tabby's hand as he hurried down the driveway, the kids at his heels. "It is beyond my comprehension how Dr. Woo expects me to do my job and babysit you two at the same time."

"We don't need a babysitter," Pearl said huffily. "We're old enough to take care of ourselves."

"I hope you are old enough to take care of yourselves, because being an apprentice for Dr. Woo will not be like working at an ice-cream parlor or in a candy shop. It will be dangerous work, I tell you. And I do not have time to watch over you."

The scars on Dr. Woo's face and neck and her missing finger were like neon warning signs. Ben remembered how the hatchling's flame had nearly burned off his face. "Maybe this isn't such a good idea," he said, common sense tugging at his thoughts. His parents wouldn't be pleased if he came home missing a foot or covered in claw marks.

"Too late for you to change your mind," Mr. Tabby told him as they reached the gate. "You have agreed. You have signed the contract of secrecy."

He raised his eyebrows and stared down at Ben. "Are you a man who keeps his word? Or are you a liar?"

"I'm not a liar," Ben said.

"Ben tells a lot of stories," Pearl said. "But that's different from lying."

"Stories?" Mr. Tabby frowned. "Well, you are forbidden to tell any of Dr. Woo's stories. Do you understand?"

Ben nodded.

"Then, if you are able to obtain your parents' permission, I shall see you here Monday at eight o'clock in the morning. Do not be late." Mr. Tabby opened the gate.

"Should we bring anything?" Pearl asked. "Like a backpack or a sack lunch?"

Mr. Tabby's nose twitched. "It is always a good idea to bring bandages. Lots and lots of bandages." He reached into his vest and pulled out two rolled-up pieces of paper, each tied neatly with a ribbon. "I almost forgot. Each of you has earned a certificate in Sasquatch Catching."

"Thanks," Ben and Pearl said as they took the certificates.

"Eight in the morning," Mr. Tabby repeated as he locked the gate behind them. "Do not be late or I shall be most displeased." Then he turned on his heels and headed back to the old factory.

"Look," Pearl whispered, nudging Ben with her elbow.

As Mr. Tabby walked away, a tail slid out from under his vest—a long red cat's tail. But it was there for only a moment, then disappeared as if...

As if it had been...imaginary.

22

THE BEST STORY EVER

Do you think we should go into the forest and check on Mrs. Mulberry and Victoria?" Ben asked.

"I guess so," Pearl said.

They hurried across the road and were just about to head up the forest path when a horn honked and a blue-and-white patrol car pulled up alongside. The darkened window rolled down, and Officer Milly stuck out her head. "Hiya, Pearl. Hiya, Ben. What are you two up to?"

"Nothing," Pearl said.

"Nothing," Ben said.

Ben's reflection stared back at him in Officer Milly's sunglasses. He looked exactly the same as he'd looked when he'd gotten up that morning. But he'd just had the most amazing adventure of his life. *Shouldn't I look different?* he wondered.

Officer Milly stared over the rims of her glasses. "It's been a strange morning. A stray dog got loose in the senior center and made a real big mess. But no one got hurt. You two wouldn't know anything about that, would you?"

"No," Pearl and Ben said.

"What about the net that was left in the forest? Do you know anything about that?"

"No," Pearl and Ben said.

"Well, Mrs. Mulberry and Victoria Mulberry got tangled in the net, but they're okay. No harm done." Officer Milly pointed to the rolled-up paper in Pearl's hand. "Whatcha got there?"

"We got jobs at the worm hospital," Pearl said.

"We're going to work Monday, Wednesday, and Friday all summer."

"What do you do at a worm hospital?" Officer Milly asked.

"Feed the worms," Ben said.

"Take them for walks," Pearl said.

"And give them baths," Ben added. "Stuff like that."

"All summer, huh?" Officer Milly chuckled. "Well, it sounds like it will keep you two out of trouble. Come on, I'll give you both a ride home."

Ben and Pearl climbed into the backseat. As they rode to Pine Street, Ben might have been thrilled about riding in the back of a police car. But his brain was flooded with images—the dragon swooping between clouds, the hatchling dangling from Barnaby's mouth, the sasquatch eating butterscotch pudding. And, of course, the tail poking out from Mr. Tabby's vest. All those things were way better than any story Ben had ever told.

"How come you two are so quiet?" Officer Milly

asked, glancing at them in the rearview mirror. "You got some secrets?"

Ben smiled at Pearl. Pearl smiled back.

Grandpa Abe was still at the senior center when Ben arrived back at his house. Barnaby was lying in wait beneath a bird feeder, swatting at chickadees. Once inside, Ben opened his sock drawer and tucked the Sasquatch Catching certificate way in the back. Monday couldn't arrive fast enough. What would happen at Dr. Woo's secret hospital? Perhaps he'd learn why the doctor had been covered in fairy dust? And who or what eats kiwi-flavored jelly beans? Perhaps he'd learn where to find the Imaginary World.

Or maybe he'd actually go there.

He scooped Snooze out of the cage and cradled him in his hands. "I think it's going to be a great summer," he told his hamster. Snooze stared at Ben with his beady black eyes. Then he curled up into a ball and fell asleep. Ben tucked Snooze back into his nest and closed the cage. Life is simple in a plastic rectangle, where nothing changes.

But sometimes change is just what life needs. Sometimes change is a very good thing.

Ben smiled. Then he headed into the kitchen to do the dishes.

PUT YOUR IMAGINATION
⚞ TO THE TEST ⚟

The following section contains writing, art, and science activities that will help readers discover more about the mythological creatures featured in this book.

These activities are designed for the home and the classroom. Enjoy doing them on your own or with friends!

CREATURE CONNE[

Stories about dragons are found all over the world, but the stories that come from Eastern cultures are very different from the stories that come from the West.

Dragons from the East tend to be friendly and helpful. They often have important lessons to teach humans, and they live peacefully. Killing one of these dragons is considered a tragedy.

The tradition in the West is to write about dangerous dragons. These fire-breathing creatures often burn villages to the ground, hoard treasure, and eat sheep, cows, and sometimes children. Stories about Western dragons tend to be about a hero who must slay the dragon to save a village or even a damsel in distress. Western dragons guard their treasure and will kill anyone who tries to take it.

The dragon hatchling that Ben found on his bed

s a wyvern. The wyvern is one type of Western dragon. It is different from other Western dragons because it has two legs rather than four. Descriptions of wyverns differ from story to story, but most describe them as ranging from muddy brown to a greenish color. Like other Western dragons, the wyvern has wings and can fly. In some stories it shoots flame, while in others it shoots poison. It is often said to have a barbed tail and a neck and head that are very snakelike. Some say wyverns come from Africa and that their favorite food is the elephant. But this dragon became very popular in the Middle Ages in Britain, especially in a region known as Wales.

Back in those days, knights would gather for tournaments, fighting one another in contests to see who would become the champion. Because knights wore heavy armor and their faces were covered by helmets, no one could tell who was who. So these knights carried flags and coats of arms to identify themselves and to honor their families—this is called heraldry. Many used the wyvern as a symbol on their flags. To wear the wyvern on your coat of arms meant that you were strong and fierce.

STORY IDEA

Imagine that you found a wyvern hatchling on your bed and you decided to keep it. You've been feeding it table scraps and hiding it in your closet, but one day you come home and discover...

ART IDEA

Pretend you are a knight in shining armor and you are going to compete in a tournament. What will your flag look like? Create your own flag using an image of the wyvern. Remember, it has two feet instead of four.

CREATURE CONNECTION
★ *Sasquatch* ★

Some people believe that there's a big creature living in the woods in the Pacific Northwest. Other people say there's no such thing.

Those who claim to have seen this creature say it's big and hairy, walks on two legs, smells bad, and leaves enormous footprints. They've taken pictures of it. But those who don't believe claim that the pictures are of people in gorilla suits. Does this creature exist?

This much we know is true—throughout history, humans have created stories about wild men and women who live in the forest. They tend to be bigger than normal men and women, hairier, and a bit scary. If you were a kid in medieval Europe, your parents might tell you about the woodwose, a hairy wild man of the woods. If you grew up in Russia, you might know about the leshy, a tall man who protects the forest. If you lived in the

Himalayas, you might go to bed hearing about the yeti, a wild man who lives in the snowy mountains. And if you lived with the Salish people of the Pacific Northwest, you might go to bed hearing about the wild man called the sésquac.

The native people of the Pacific Northwest had so many stories about wild men that someone decided to collect these stories. His name was J. W. Burns. In the 1920s, he worked as a teacher on the Chehalis Indian Reservation, and after he'd collected the stories, he wrote a newspaper article called "Introducing British Columbia's Hairy Giants." Mr. Burns is the person who invented the word *sasquatch*. There were many different native names for the wild-man creature, and Mr. Burns wanted to simplify things, so he created one name.

Later, in the 1950s, a bunch of footprints were found in northern California. When a photo of these footprints appeared in the newspaper the *Humboldt Times*, the writer decided to call the creature bigfoot, and that is how the sasquatch got its nickname.

Today, there are many websites and even a television show dedicated to finding the sasquatch. In Seattle, a publishing company and a music festival are named after the hairy beast.

STORY IDEAS

Pretend you are sitting around a fire a very long time ago and you are the storyteller for your village. You don't want the little children to go into the woods, because the woods are filled with wolves and bears. So you must tell the children a story that will keep them out of the woods. You tell them about a strange creature that...

★ ★ ★ ★ ★

Pretend you are a newspaper reporter and you've just heard that someone in your town has found a giant footprint. You grab your notebook, pen, and camera and hurry to the location. But when you get there, you find something else....

ART IDEA

Draw different kinds of footprints. A person, a cat, a dog, a bird—whatever you'd like—but be sure to include a sasquatch. Think about how the footprints compare in size and shape.

SCIENCE CONNECTION
★ *Dragon's Milk* ★

In our story, Mr. Tabby had a recipe for a concoction he called Artificial Dragon's Milk. It's a recipe he perfected over the years to give to young dragons when no fresh meat was available. But dragons are supposed to be reptiles, right? And reptiles don't drink milk, do they? So why did the baby wyvern drink milk?

Reptiles include snakes, lizards, turtles, tortoises, alligators, crocodiles, and the extinct dinosaurs.

Reptiles are cold-blooded animals. This means that they have to rely on the outside world to heat or cool their bodies. So if a reptile wants to get warm, it lies in the sun. If it wants to cool down, it hides under a rock or floats in the water. Reptile bodies do not maintain a consistent temperature the way mammal bodies do.

Reptiles have scales (snakes), shields (tortoises),

or plates (crocodiles) covering their bodies. And all baby reptiles are hatched from eggs. Most of the time, the eggs are laid, but in a few cases, such as with the garter snake, the egg is kept inside the mother's body until it hatches, and then the baby snake emerges.

So why don't reptiles drink milk?

Milk comes from mammals. Baby mammals are not able to take care of themselves when they are born. They would die without a mother or father to feed them. So a mother mammal makes milk, which she feeds to her baby.

But baby reptiles are independent the moment they are born. This means they slither or crawl or swim away from their parents and seek food on their own. A mother or father reptile does not need to provide food. How much easier it is to be a reptile parent—once the kids are hatched, you're free!

So back to the question, why did the baby wyvern drink milk? Dragons are reptiles, but they are also magical creatures, so the regular rules don't apply to them. This is why a baby dragon might drink milk—or else it might eat your neighbor!

STORY IDEAS

Imagine two mothers, a snake mother and a squirrel mother, are sitting in the garden talking about their babies. How are their lives different?

★ ★ ★ ★ ★

Imagine you are a baby dragon, just emerging from the shell. What does it feel like to break through the shell? What does your world look like? What is the first thing you do?

CREATIVITY CONNECTION
★ *Make Your Own Homemade Pudding* ★

Here is a supereasy recipe for homemade chocolate pudding. You make it in the microwave, so you don't have to worry about using a hot stove. Be sure to have a parent or grown-up help you.

Here's what you need:

> ¼ cup cornstarch
> ¼ cup cocoa powder (Don't use unsweetened cocoa powder. If you want it extra chocolaty, use dark cocoa powder.)
> ½ cup sugar
> 2¼ cups whole milk
> 1 teaspoon vanilla extract
> 2 tablespoons butter (Don't use margarine.)

★ ★ ★ ★ ★

1. Mix the cornstarch, cocoa, and sugar in a big bowl that is microwave-safe. You want a big bowl because during the last cooking step the pudding will bubble, and you don't want it to bubble over the sides.

2. Add the milk. Stir. Don't worry, it will be lumpy.

3. Heat in the microwave for two minutes. The bowl will be hot, so use an oven mitt to remove the bowl from the microwave. Stir the pudding with a whisk.

4. Heat for two more minutes. Remove with an oven mitt. Stir with the whisk. Everything should be melted now, and the pudding should look like hot chocolate.

5. Heat again for two minutes. The bowl

will be extra hot, so be careful. Now your pudding is thick. Stir with the whisk, making sure there are no lumps.

6. Add the vanilla and butter. Stir again with the whisk. The butter will melt while you stir. The pudding is thicker now.

7. Ladle or pour the hot pudding into little serving cups. Press plastic wrap onto the top of the pudding to keep a skin from forming. Put the cups in the refrigerator.

When the pudding has cooled, it's ready to eat!

ACKNOWLEDGMENTS

Huge thanks to Michael Bourret, Julie Scheina, Pam Garfinkel, Christine Ma, and everyone at Little, Brown for helping me launch this fun new series. For help with the Yiddish, I called upon librarian Janine Rosenbaum and my dear friend Gary Pazoff, who got his uncle Stew on the phone just to make sure. Yiddish dictionaries differ greatly, so I chose the spellings that I felt would be most familiar to readers.

Big thanks to Dan Santat for capturing my story in his gorgeous illustrations.

And, as always, big hugs and kisses to Bob, Isabelle, and Walker for all their love, support, and tiptoeing.

I love hearing from readers, so please visit me at www.suzanneselfors.com.